"Are you sure you want to do this?"

Blake had parked across from the precinct but he knew they should be running.

"I have to. I can't be involved in this." Holly looked at him, her eyes searching his. "What are you going to do?"

"My best to get out of this town alive."

She nodded, then opened the car door. She had one leg out when he stopped her. "Wait." He was surprised by the intensity of his feelings for her, and in such a short time.

She looked back at him, but his words caught in his throat. He should say something to help her but every instinct was telling him this wasn't right. "Please don't do this," he said. "You're making a mistake by going in there."

"I'll be fine," she assured him, exiting the car.

He watched her enter the police station, his heart hammering against his chest. Had he rescued her hours ago from a killer only to let her walk into the lion's den?

Virginia Vaughan is a born-and-raised Mississippi girl. She is blessed to come from a large Southern family, and her fondest memories include listening to stories recounted around the dinner table. She was a lover of books from a young age, devouring tales of romance, danger and love. She soon started writing them herself. You can connect with Virginia through her website, virginiavaughanonline.com, or through the publisher.

Books by Virginia Vaughan

Love Inspired Suspense

Rangers Under Fire

Yuletide Abduction
Reunion Mission
Ranch Refuge
Mistletoe Reunion Threat
Mission Undercover

No Safe Haven

MISSION UNDERCOVER

VIRGINIA VAUGHAN

HARLEQUIN® LOVE INSPIRED® SUSPENSE

LOVE INSPIRED BOOKS

Recycling programs
for this product may
not exist in your area.

ISBN-13: 978-0-373-45725-0

Mission Undercover

Copyright © 2017 by Virginia Vaughan

www.Harlequin.com

Printed in U.S.A.

The pride of man will be humbled
and the loftiness of men will be abased;
And the Lord alone will be exalted in that day.
–Isaiah 2:17

This book is lovingly dedicated to my Lord and Savior Jesus Christ through whom all things are possible. And to the two little boys who have recently changed my life. Raising little ones again was not in my plan, but thankfully God had a different, wonderful path for us all.

ONE

Blake Michaels pulled into the parking lot of Northshore Medical Center and cut the engine. He spotted Mason Webber's police cruiser a few rows away. Mason was sitting behind the wheel. Blake reached for his pistol and tucked it into the waistband of his jeans. He didn't know what Mason wanted, but he suspected it couldn't be good.

He and Mason weren't on the best of terms and his call asking Blake to meet him had been cryptic. Besides, Blake had gotten used to trusting no one. That's what made this job perfect for him. After his fiancée Miranda had betrayed him, distrust came easily to him. And he had a lot of reasons to distrust the town's police force, especially Mason Webber.

Blake got out, pulled his shirt over his weapon and then headed for Mason's cruiser. The sound of jackhammers reached his ears, but he realized it was only construction happening outside the hospital.

He slid into the passenger's seat of the police car

and immediately saw the folder lying on the console between them. A folder with his name written on it.

That could not be good.

Mason noticed him gaze at the folder and his lip quirked as if he found the entire matter amusing. He smacked his hand against the steering wheel. "I learned something about you today, Blakey," he said, using a nickname Blake absolutely detested. "You're not who you claim to be."

He held his breath. Had Mason discovered his real reason for joining the Northshore Police Department? He wanted to keep his voice casual but his mouth was bone-dry with apprehension. He'd known men like Mason during his time as an Army Ranger. Their macho bravado hid insecurities that were highlighted when a gun and bullets was added to the mix.

Mason reached for the folder and tossed it at Blake. It fell open and his photo, along with what looked like his police service record, spilled out. Blake picked up one sheet of paper and saw that it was his police service file—his *real* service file. How had Mason gotten his hands on it? "Where did this come from?"

"I have powerful friends in this town." Fire blazed in his eyes and his hand gripped the gun in his lap. "You're investigating us."

Knowing Mason was already on edge, Blake would have to choose his words carefully. He'd already spent months trying to find out just who these "powerful friends" were, but hadn't had much success. The men he'd met on the Northshore PD, including Mason Webber, liked to do a lot of bragging, but they were surprisingly tight-lipped for dirty cops.

"Who gave you this?" Blake asked. His official record had been supposedly altered by the Department of Justice when he'd accepted this undercover assignment in Northshore, Arkansas. So how had someone gotten their hands on his real-life info?

"You're investigating me. In fact, you're investigating this whole department."

It was a statement, not a question, and Blake couldn't refute it. That didn't mean he wouldn't try. "I'm investigating the drug ring. That's all I care about, Mason. You don't have to be a part of this." That wasn't entirely the truth, but he needed Mason to think he had an out if he would just take it.

"I already am. Your cover is blown at the precinct. The boss knows all about you, Blake Michaels. Now you've got not only the drug ring after you, but Northshore PD, as well."

But who is the guy in charge?

That was the question Blake had spent months trying to figure out. He suspected it was someone working in the Northshore PD, and probably someone high up. In fact, the DOJ surmised that as many as twenty-five police officers—probably more—were involved in the massive drug ring operating out of the small town. And that was the real reason Blake had joined the department—and why he was sitting in Mason's car now.

His friend Matt had landed him the gig with the DEA/DOJ combined task force. The agencies had been looking to send in someone with proven law-enforcement experience to pretend to be dirty and to gather information. Blake had the police background and had been in serious need of a change after being betrayed by his fiancée. Only he hadn't been able to gather much intel even after nine months here.

Mason perked up as he saw something through the windshield. Blake followed his line of sight and noticed a pretty, dark-haired woman in scrubs leaving the employee entrance of the hospital. He didn't recognize her, but her hair was around her face and her walk weary, making Blake assume she had just finished her shift at the hospital.

"Who is she?" Blake asked.

"Her name is Holly Mathis. She was Jimmy's wife."

Blake knew Mason's partner, Jim Mathis, had been shot and killed nearly a year ago while responding to a burglary in progress at a gas station. The shooter had also been killed.

He didn't know what Holly Mathis had to do with this, though he didn't like the look in Mason's eyes or the coincidence that Mason had brought him here to drop his bombshell just as his former partner's widow was leaving work.

"Why are we here, Mason?"

"I just wanted you both in the same place. It makes it easier."

Blake's heart hammered in his chest. "Easier to do what?"

Mason picked up his gun and pointed it at Blake. "To kill you both."

Sweat broke out on Blake's brow, but he forced himself to remain calm. His life depended on it. He stared down the barrel of the gun, caught off guard by this sudden change. He scanned the area, realizing Mason had chosen the perfect spot for this ambush. He looked past the gun to Mason's face. "And your boss, whoever that is, sent you here to kill me?"

"Yep. Then I'm going to kill Holly, too. I can see tomorrow's headline now—Obsessed Police Officer Murders Girlfriend then Kills Himself."

"Why her? Why kill Holly? She's your partner's widow. You should be looking out for her."

His jaw tightened and his eyes narrowed in anger. "She betrayed me just like you did."

Blake tried another tactic. "You'll have to make my death look like a suicide in order to make that work and a direct shot won't do it. The coroner will know I didn't shoot myself. There will be an investigation."

Mason laughed, a humorless chuckle. "Not if the coroner is in our pocket, he won't. He'll do what the boss says. I hear he's got a little drug problem he's been trying to keep under wraps. Fortunately for him, we keep him well supplied, so he'll say whatever we want him to say."

Blake knew he couldn't reach his gun before Mason fired. He had to think of another way out of this car and he had to do it fast.

"Did you really believe you could come to my town and deceive everyone?" Mason's tone held bitterness and betrayal, as if Blake's deception had been directed only toward him.

Blake slid his hand behind him and felt for the door handle. The situation was bad and he had to find a way out of it. He'd already been ambushed by this maniac and Holly was next. He also needed to let Matt and the DEA know his cover had been blown before the drug ring shut down and covered its tracks.

But as Mason rattled on about his betrayal of their trust, Blake's own anger burned. What did Mason Webber know about betrayal? He hadn't had his heart ripped out by someone he loved. He hadn't had to deal with knowing his fiancée was responsible for placing those he cared about in danger and nearly getting his best friend shot to death. But this wasn't the time for that discussion. He wouldn't wish that kind of betrayal on his worst enemy—not even Mason.

"And what about her?" Blake asked. "I've never met her before in my life. How are you going to explain that?"

"Won't be too hard to make it look like you two were together. Just another obsessed cop taking out his frustrations on his girl. They'll probably make us all take more domestic violence seminars again because of it and the department will suffer some bad press—but we'll get through it."

So he had it all planned out. And if the coroner was in fact dirty, as Mason claimed, no one in this town would question their deaths. But Matt and the other Rangers would. They knew him too well to believe such a crazy concoction.

"Killing me would be a mistake," Blake warned him.

"You have powerful friends, but so do I. They'll swarm this town and take you all down."

Mason took only a moment to ponder that statement before he braced his arm, a sign Blake knew meant he was about to fire. In one swift move, Blake reached for his gun and pushed open the door, tumbling backward and rolling from the car as Mason fired twice. Blake felt the whiz of one bullet pass inches from his head while the other bit into his side as he tumbled. He hit the pavement, jamming his shoulder. He immediately rolled beneath the car as Mason jumped out the driver's door and ran around to find him. When he did, Blake slid out the other side and hightailed it through the lot, staying low to use the cars as cover.

Mason swore then started searching for him, calling out his name. "Come out, come out, Blakey. I'll find you sooner or later."

Blake stopped and leaned against a car, his breathing labored and perspiration rolling off him. His shoulder ached but that wasn't his most pressing concern. He touched his stomach and his hand came back bloody. He was hurt and he was leaving a blood trail behind him for Mason to follow. He had to get to his car, get as far away from Mason as possible and figure this all out. If Mason was to be believed, he was now being hunted by both the police and a powerful drug ring.

Lord, don't forsake me now.

He adjusted the grip of his gun. If he was going down, he would go down fighting.

"You can't get away," Mason called to him. "I know I hit you. You're bleeding bad. And soon you'll have the entire police force hunting you. You won't make it out of this town alive."

Blake sucked in a breath and took off, again staying low so Mason wouldn't see him. After a few minutes, he stopped to catch his breath one more time. He leaned against a Prius and listened for Mason's footsteps. He was shocked to realize they were heading away from him instead of toward him.

He peeked around the front of the car and saw Mason moving through the parking lot—just as he'd suspected—away from him.

He glanced in the direction Mason was headed. Holly was approaching her car and Mason was moving to intercept her.

A rush of panic shot through him.

Mason had left him and was going after the girl.

He clutched his gun and forced himself to his feet, new energy pulsing through him. He couldn't...he wouldn't...let Mason kill her.

Holly Mathis rubbed her shoulder, trying to work out the kinks in her muscles. The sounds of the construction by the employee's entrance hurt her head. Why did they have to make so much noise? She couldn't even hear herself think. It had been another long night at the hospital and she was looking forward to a hot bath and then crawling into bed. She was tired, but at least it helped keep her mind free from the worry that had occupied her thoughts recently. If she gave herself time to focus on what she'd found and its implications, she might drive herself crazy.

Why didn't you tell me, Jimmy?

Her husband's death twelve months ago had left her life shattered and in confusion, but slowly, surely, she'd begun to live again…until two days ago when she'd been cleaning out the closet and discovered the hidden compartment and the leather-bound journal inside. What was written there had rocked her world and sent her reeling back into that place where thoughts of Jimmy occupied her every thought.

Had he died in the line of duty as his partner had claimed? She was beginning to question it. Her first instinct upon finding the journal had been to take it to Jimmy's chief, but something had stopped her, some invisible hand—Jimmy's? God's?—on her soul had warned her to be cautious with what she shared.

Instead she'd photocopied a few pages that highlighted Mason's wrongdoings and showed them to the chief. He'd been interested, pressing her to bring in the rest of the book, and Holly thought he'd seemed agitated even as he was trying to appear calm. But she'd seen sweat on his brow. He'd been unsettled about Jimmy's findings, but what police chief wouldn't be shaken after seeing evidence indicating he had a dirty cop on his force?

And Mason's numerous visits made sense now, too. He'd become increasingly obsessed with her since Jimmy's death. His constant calls and visits at the hospital and her home had bordered on harassment. She'd thought several times about filing a complaint with Chief Waggoner, but had hoped the problem would go away on its own and Mason would find someone else to focus his attention on.

Her attempts to appease Mason hadn't worked and she knew why. He hadn't really been obsessed with her. He'd been looking for information about what she knew of her husband's investigation. Well, Mason needn't have worried. Jimmy had kept his suspicions all to himself and hadn't told her anything about corruption on the force. He'd seemed anxious and stressed in the last few weeks of his life, but he hadn't given her any clue as to why when she'd questioned him about his behavior.

She'd been ready to turn the journal over to Chief Waggoner until yesterday when she'd arrived home to find her house had been broken into and trashed. It had been obvious that whoever had broken in had been searching for something—Jimmy's journal she'd assumed—but when she'd checked the secret hiding spot, it had still been there. They hadn't found it. The break-in couldn't have been a coincidence, which left her wondering how Mason had found out about the journal in the first place.

What do I do now?

She didn't know who she was talking to—Jimmy? Or God? She hadn't spoken to God in nearly a year, not after He'd taken her husband from her and left her a widow. But she let the question float out there and hoped for an answer. She sighed as she pulled her keys from her purse. Maybe she was reading too much into this and the break-in at her house had nothing to do with Jimmy's journal, after all.

She reached to unlock her car door, stopping when

she spotted the shadow of a man in the window. Her heart leaped at the sight, but her instincts kicked in. She ducked, causing him to miss as he reached to grab her and hit the window instead. She spun around to face him.

Mason!

He raised his gun at her and words of protest caught in her throat. Fear rippled through her. At this close distance she could smell the acrid, sulfur aroma that indicated he'd fired his weapon recently. Very recently.

"Hello, Holly," he snarled, his face contorted and bitter.

She saw murder in his eyes and knew she was in trouble. Jimmy had taught her about guns and had even bought her one for safety before he'd died, but the hospital had a strict no-guns policy so it was safely locked inside her car—so close but so out of reach. She had to find a way to get to it.

She raised her hands, palms out, in a take-it-easy kind of gesture. "Mason, what are you doing? Put the gun down."

He shook his head. "No, Holly. Tell me where the book is."

"I—I don't know what you're talking about."

"We both know that's a lie." He pulled a folded piece of paper from his pocket and threw it on the ground. She saw that it was one of the copied pages of the journal.

"Where did you get that?"

"Did you think you could hide it from me? Tell me where the book is, Holly, and I'll kill you quickly. Don't tell me and I'll kill you slowly and find it anyway."

He gripped the gun tighter and Holly felt her blood go cold. This was it. This was where she was going to die. But she wouldn't give him what he wanted.

"You'll never find it," she whispered and saw his face contort. Tears warmed her eyes and she began to shake. She choked them back and prepared to fight for her life, but before she could act, another man—this one broad and muscular—leaped from behind a car and tackled Mason as he fired.

Holly dived for the ground as the blast of the gun rang in her ears. She scrambled for cover in front of the car then peeked around the bumper to see Mason and the other man hit the ground. The gun slipped from Mason's hand and spun across the asphalt beneath her car. Holly considered crawling after it, but Mason and her rescuer were in the way. The broad-shouldered man was on top of Mason. He punched him and Mason slumped to the ground.

The man crawled to his feet and looked around, spotting her crouched behind a parked car. Using his sleeve, he wiped sweat from his brow and then held out his hand to her. "Don't be afraid. My name is Blake Michaels. I'm here to help you." Urgency poured from him as Mason began to squirm, mere moments from regaining consciousness. "We have to go. Now."

Holly took his outstretched hand and let him pull her to her feet, but she hesitated at following him, glancing at her car. Should she try to get past Mason to retrieve her gun and cell phone?

"He wants you dead," Blake said matter-of-factly, interrupting her indecision. "He wants us both dead.

Now, let's get out of here before he comes to and finishes the job he started."

She glanced back at Mason, still trying to pull himself awake. He'd come to kill her tonight and he almost had. This man, whoever he was, had saved her life.

She nodded and followed him to a Dodge Ram pickup. He unlocked the doors and she slid across the seat as he got in on the driver's side. Holly spotted blood on his hands as he started the engine. Her gaze moved to his midsection, where a dark circle was growing on his shirt.

"You're hurt," she stated as he took off. "What happened?"

He waved away her concern. "It's nothing. The bullet just grazed me."

"I'm a nurse. I should take a look at it."

"Maybe later. First we have to get as far away from Mason Webber as possible."

She looked at the handsome stranger who had saved her life and shuddered. Mason had shot him, actually shot him, proving that he was even more dangerous than Holly had wanted to admit.

How do I get myself into these situations?

"Okay, so I know what he has against me. Why does he want you dead, Blake Michaels?"

"That is a long story." He moved his hand from the steering wheel and felt along the seat as he drove. "Do you see my cell phone anywhere?"

Holly glanced around but didn't see it. "No."

He slammed his hand against the steering wheel. "I must have dropped it. Do you have a phone?"

"No. We're not allowed to bring them inside during our shifts. It's locked inside my car." *Along with my gun.* She sighed, wishing she had both right now.

He didn't slow down as they approached the turn-off for the police precinct. In fact, he drove right by it. "Aren't we going to the police station? We need to let them know what just happened tonight."

He shook his head but didn't let up on the accelerator. "We can't go to the police."

"Why not? I know Mason is a cop but he's out of his mind. The chief needs to know he's dangerous."

"I said no police." His voice was sharp and biting.

He was so insistent that it caused her to wonder why he was wary of police involvement. She realized she didn't even know this man she'd gotten into a truck with. "Why don't you want to go to the police? Are you a criminal?"

"No, I'm a cop." He reached into his back pocket and pulled out his wallet, flipping it open on the seat. She saw a badge and breathed a sigh of relief.

When she picked it up, something fell out. She reached down and picked it up. It was a ring…an engagement ring. She glanced at him but he hadn't noticed the ring slip out. He was busy checking the mirrors. She slipped the ring back into his wallet and examined the badge. His name was written on his credentials. Blake Michaels, Northshore Police. Okay, so maybe he wasn't a criminal, but she still didn't know anything about him except that he didn't trust his fellow officers and he carried an engagement ring around with him.

"If you're one of them, then why not go to the cops?"

"Because Mason wasn't working alone. The force is corrupt. We can't trust anyone."

She gasped. Corrupt cops? How did he know? Jimmy had suspected as much before he died. In fact, he'd been looking into acts of corruption by his partner, according to the journal she'd discovered. Mason had seemed to have no fear of reprimand in his behavior tonight. But was the entire department really so corrupt that they could ignore attempted murder?

"So if we're not going to the police, where are we going?"

"We need to get out of town fast, out of their jurisdiction."

Getting to the next town was a sensible idea. They could sort this all out once they were there. She noticed the spot on his shirt growing larger. "You'll never make it. You're bleeding too badly. My friend Marcy's apartment is a few blocks over. I know where she hides the emergency key. We should go there first so I can take a look at your wound."

He shook his head. "That's not a good idea."

"You're going to bleed out before we hit the town line and it's at least five miles before we'll find a place to get supplies. Marcy's a nurse, too. She'll have bandages there."

"I don't want to put anyone else in danger."

She shook her head. "Neither Marcy or her roommate are at home now. They both went on duty as I was getting off."

He grimaced at the pain then nodded his agreement. "We can't stay long."

She directed him to the apartment and he parked behind the building. "In case he drives by," he explained.

When they got out, Holly noticed him holding his hand over his wound. He looked pale and she wondered if he could even make it up the stairs. "It's on the second floor. I'll help you up."

He waved away her offer of assistance. "I'll make it." He leaned on the handrail and followed her up the steps.

Looking at the blood on his shirt and hands, she didn't know how he was standing and suspected his wound was more than a graze. She hoped he didn't have a bullet lodged in his abdomen or damage to his internal organs. She wouldn't know until she could examine the wound.

Holly found the emergency key under a planter and used it to unlock the door. She ushered Blake inside. "Have a seat on the couch. I'll go get the first-aid kit."

"Is there a phone here?"

She shook her head. "No landline. Marcy and her roommate use their cell phones."

She hurried down the hall to the bathroom and grabbed the kit and a stack of towels, stopping to catch her breath before returning to the living room. This was all happening so fast and now her protector, the man who'd saved her, might be seriously injured. She had to help him.

He was stretched out on the couch when she returned, his long legs hanging over one end and his gun now on the table inches from his hand. She was struck by his long, muscular frame and a pang of envy rushed through her as she remembered the ring inside his wallet.

He reached out and touched her arm, a soft, gentle touch that sent a spark of electricity through her. "Are you okay?"

She smiled, realizing he was the one hurt and yet was concerned about her. What would it be like to have a brave, handsome man like Blake in her life? She knew the answer to that. She'd had one…and she'd lost him in the line of duty. She'd hardly given romance a second thought since Jimmy's death. But now, as she realized how close she'd come to her life ending, she acknowledged the deep longing ache in her heart for someone to share her life with. Her husband's death had ended her dream, but she was still young and many of her friends had pressed her to start dating again.

"I'm fine," she said, determined not to let her vulnerability show and convinced the trauma of the past hour was causing her emotions to go wacky.

She knelt beside him and shifted into nurse mode. She lifted his shirt, wiping away blood so she could see the wound. Thankfully, he'd been right. The gash wasn't big enough for the bullet to have gone in. "It must have grazed you. It's not even that deep."

"Why is it bleeding so much?"

"Because you're moving around and because of where the wound is. You could probably use some stitches, but we'll have to make do." She cleaned him off then taped a bandage over it. "You're fortunate it was only a flesh wound. It could have been much worse."

"I know. He took me by surprise. He meant to kill me." He sat up and stared at her, his blue eyes piercing as he looked her in the eye. "He meant to kill us both."

She nodded, realizing he was right. Mason wanted her dead. The thought shook her. She was used to seeing the effects of violence in her job as an ER nurse, but this was different. This was personal. "You still haven't told me why he wants you dead."

She picked up discarded bandage wrappers as he pulled down his shirt and sat up. "He found out I've been investigating him. There's a major drug operation happening in Northshore. I believe Mason and several other officers are involved in it. Mason said someone high up was involved."

"How high up?"

"High enough to pay off the coroner so he'd classify our deaths as a murder/suicide after Mason killed us."

She gasped, stunned by his bravado. "He really said that?"

He nodded then stood and walked to the window, glancing out. "The thing is, I don't know who to trust on the force. Everyone is suspect."

"Do you really believe there's that much corruption?"

"It's a small-town force. Most of these boys grew up here and have known one another since birth. They're wary of outsiders. There are only a handful from out of town and that was only after Mayor Banks ran on the platform of improving police procedures. She wanted college graduates with more criminal justice education and insisted the city offer them leadership positions. Only two of us are still around. The others got fed up with small-town politics and left."

She nodded, remembering the mayor's platform. Jimmy had been taking night classes to finish his degree and he'd hoped to nab one of those supervisory spots. But he'd been killed before finishing. And she wasn't surprised so many had gotten fed up and left. "Why would so many accept a job in Northshore?"

He turned to look at her and she thought she saw pain flash through his eyes. "Some like the idea of joining the force with some influence. Some who've worked in the big city are looking for the slower-paced life. Others just needed a change."

His expression told her instinctively he'd been one of the ones who'd needed a change. Something had happened to him, something that had wounded him deeply. Did it have something to do with that ring he carried around?

Blake's investigation into corruption among his fellow officers showed he had integrity. She respected that he'd made a vow to this town and this police force to clean it up and he was following through.

"I need to change my clothes," she said, getting up and walking down the hallway toward the bedroom. She shut the door and leaned against it, closing her eyes and wishing this all away. She discarded her scrubs and slipped into a pair of Marcy's jeans and a blouse she borrowed from her closet. Thankfully, they wore the same size. She moved to the bathroom and leaned into the sink as anger pulsed through her.

Only a few days after the funeral, Mason and a few other officers had come to their house and toted away boxes of information they'd claimed were part of an investigation. She hadn't realized it at the time, but now she knew that Mason had been at the center of Jimmy's investigation. And she'd let him walk out with her husband's work. As if that wasn't bad enough, he was now trying to kill her. And she was trapped with a man she didn't even know. He claimed to be one of the good guys and he seemed to have the same mission her husband had had—ferreting out corruption among the police—but she didn't know Blake Michaels and had no idea if she could trust him or not.

"What should I do?" She whispered the question to Jimmy. When no apparent answer presented itself, she moved from the bathroom to the bedroom door and cracked it open. She could see Blake standing guard at the window.

Her instincts said she could trust Blake, and she had little choice right now. She would go with him and let the state police worry about who was corrupt and who wasn't.

She walked into the living room and he turned from the window.

"How are you feeling?" he asked, his eyes sincere and full of concern.

"I'm fine. Everything is just happening so fast."

"I know. It's a lot to take in."

She handed him a clean shirt. "I found this in Marcy's closet. It's probably her boyfriend's shirt, but it should fit you and it's clean. You can change in the bathroom."

"Thank you." He disappeared down the hall then returned a moment later having discarded the blood soaked shirt and buttoning up the one she'd given him.

She couldn't help noticing the nice lines of his shoulders and felt herself blush. Yet before she could even chide herself for noticing, a noise outside stopped her. Blake hurried back to the window and his jaw clenched.

"It's Mason."

She ran to the window. "What? How did he know we were here?"

"I don't know, but he did. Let's get out of here."

She grabbed the first-aid kit and stuffed it into her purse in case Blake's wound needed to be redressed. She ran for the door. Blake followed behind her.

Blake started the engine, taking off as Mason came plowing down the back steps. When he reached the bottom, he raised his gun and fired.

"Shot!" she screamed then ducked in the seat. The bullet missed the truck and she realized they were too far out of range. "He'll be back," Holly said. "He probably went to get his car."

Blake didn't let up on the accelerator. "We'll be long gone before that. The bridge is the closest way out of town."

She nodded. "Good idea." Even injured he had a good head on his shoulders.

She sat back in her seat, reached for the seat belt and tried to control her breathing. They were going to be fine. They would be home free once they reached the bridge and passed the town limits sign on the other side.

After that, everything would be fine. She would tell the state police or FBI about Jimmy's journal and they could retrieve it themselves. Mason would be arrested and the other corrupt cops on the force would be identified and taken down.

Except that Mason didn't seem to care about things

like the law or jurisdictions. He would definitely pursue them even past the city limits.

Blake slowed the truck, pulling Holly back to the present. She saw why he'd slowed. The bridge entrance was blocked by a row of police cars and officers.

"Anyone you know?" she asked.

"Oh, yeah."

"Can you trust them?"

He put the truck into Reverse and backed up. "I'm not going to wait around to find out." He jerked the Dodge into Drive and took off. "We'll find another way out of town."

She knew there were only two roads out of town. The access road that led to the highway and the bridge over the lake. The town was basically cut off due to the water. If the police had blocked the bridge, she was certain the access road would also be blocked.

A few minutes later she was proved right.

Blake slowed as they approached the access road that led to the highway. It was blocked by officers.

She tensed as he once again turned around and headed back into town.

Their only escape routes were blocked.

They were trapped.

TWO

"**I** need to go to the police."

"You can't."

She turned those wide green eyes on him and Blake saw panic in them. She was trying to keep it together but he could tell she was on the verge of losing control. He saw her mind working, questioning whether or not he was going to keep her from leaving and probably wondering how she was going to get out of the Dodge and out of his grasp.

She wasn't his prisoner, but she needed to understand the danger she was in…the danger they were both in. He knew Mason well enough to know he wouldn't stop. He'd made an attempt on their lives. He had no choice now but to finish them.

His gaze continually scanned the area on the lookout for police cars. He needed to develop a plan—starting with finding a phone he could use. He had to call Matt and alert him that his cover had been blown and he was trapped. Matt and the DEA could help him come up with an escape plan.

He glanced at Holly. She looked distraught now but she'd acted admirably and he'd been impressed. He knew she was scared. She didn't want to be a part of this, but he wasn't the one who'd dragged her into it. Mason had pulled her in, and it was up to Blake to keep her safe. He could see how Mason could become obsessed with her. Tall and athletic, her long neck accentuated a lovely heart-shaped face and big green eyes, a supple mouth and a chin that jutted stubbornly in defiance. He checked himself before he focused too much on her beauty.

Yes, she was beautiful, but he couldn't allow himself to go down that road. He was still nursing a broken heart. Miranda had gone far beyond the normal everyday betrayal of having an affair or leaving him. She'd actually kidnapped his best friend Colton's girlfriend, Laura, and handed her over to a loan shark who'd planned to kill her. And she'd done it only for money. Greed had been her downfall. Greed and an unexpressed loathing of the small-town life he loved. She'd paid the ultimate price for her betrayal, though. She'd been shot and killed by the very loan shark she'd helped. How could he have been so blind? How could he have not seen her real feelings? He was still struggling with it, even after all this time, and knew he could never put his heart on the line again.

"You can't trust the police," Blake told her.

"Mason, sure. But I've known most of these people for years. Chief Waggoner has been good to me. I should have told him about Mason sooner. He deserves to know what he's done. He'll take care of it. I'll go there, tell my story, and they'll arrest Mason."

"Mason isn't going to let you go. You're a witness to an attempted murder. You're taking an awful big risk that the higher-ups aren't on Mason's side. The cops are blocking the roads out of town. Who do you think ordered that?"

"Because they've only heard Mason's side of the story. We need to go there and tell them the truth." She jutted her chin stubbornly. "I've made up my mind. I'm going to the police." Her face softened. "I am grateful to you for saving my life today, but I don't know you, Blake. I trust Chief Waggoner. He's been good to me since Jimmy died."

"Mason said people higher up were involved, high enough to pay off a coroner to cover up a murder. Don't you think the chief of police would have to be involved in something that big?"

"You're asking me to trust someone I just met over someone I've known for years—someone my husband knew and trusted with his life."

He hoped to change her mind but could see she was determined. He couldn't blame her. She had only his word that the police department was corrupt and they'd only just met. For all she knew, he was the dirty cop.

"Fine," he said, turning the truck around. "I still believe this is a bad idea, but you're not my prisoner. I'll drop you at the police station."

"It would be more believable if you would come in with me and explain what happened."

He shook his head. "I can't do that. My only chance now is to get out of town."

He parked across the street from the precinct and scoped the area. "I don't see Mason's cruiser, so I think you're okay." He looked at her, wishing he could say something that would change her mind. But she was right. This was her town. He was the outsider. And maybe she was right about Chief Waggoner. He had to concede he only had Mason's word that the higher-ups were corrupt. "Are you sure you want to do this?"

She nodded. "I have to. I can't be involved in this." She looked at him, her green eyes searching his. "What are you going to do?"

"Find somewhere to hole up, call my friends and do my best to get out of this town alive."

She nodded and then smiled at him. "Goodbye, Blake Michaels."

"Goodbye, Holly. It was nice to know you."

She opened the door and had one leg out when his hand shot out to stop her, grabbing her elbow. "Wait."

He was surprised by the intensity of his feelings for her and his hesitancy to let her go. She'd held up well against circumstances that would make a grown man lash out. He understood her need to try, but it didn't stop his concern for her safety.

She looked back at him, waiting, but his words caught in his throat. He should say something to help her, but every inch of his instinct was telling him something wasn't right. "Please don't do this," he said. "You're making a mistake by going in there."

Her smile said he was being overly cautious. "I'll

be fine," she assured him. "You'll need to change that bandage often or else you'll get an infection." She slid out of the car and crossed the street.

He watched her go, his heart hammering against his chest. He'd saved her from Mason only to have her walk into the lion's den.

Lord, please protect her.

Holly stopped at the doors to the police station and looked back. Blake's truck was gone. She sighed, already missing his protective presence.

Stop it, she chastised herself. She didn't need his protection. But she had needed it today and he'd given it freely—and been wounded himself. She should have wished him well or said she would pray for him, but the words hadn't come. She wasn't on good enough terms with God to even pray for someone else.

Besides, she didn't know Blake. Maybe he didn't deserve her prayers or her good wishes. But she found that hard to believe. He struck her as one of the good guys. He'd risked his life to save her from Mason and that spoke volumes. But she had to think logically. Reason told her she couldn't discount all of the police on the word of one man or because of Mason's actions.

I hope I'm doing the right thing.

She pushed open the door and stepped inside the precinct. The chill of the air-conditioning hit her, a nice change from the muggy midmorning temperature. The room was full of desks and people in uniform. Holly approached the front desk, where the officer on duty was hunched over the computer.

"Can I help you, lady?" he asked without looking up.

"I'd like to see Chief Waggoner."

"He's busy. Someone kidnapped a nurse over at the medical center. He's coordinating the response team."

Surprise rushed through her. Mason had claimed she'd been kidnapped? That certainly explained the police roadblocks out of town. "Then he'll definitely want to see me," she stated.

"Why? Who are you?" he asked, turning to look at her.

She waited a moment, wondering if he would recognize her. He gave her a quizzical look then his eyes widened. He jumped to his feet. "You—you're…you're her."

"That's right. Only I wasn't abducted." Indignation soared through her that Mason had made such a ridiculous claim in order to manipulate the police into a manhunt for Blake.

He nodded then picked up the phone. "I'll call Chief Waggoner."

Moments later the chief—a heavyset man in his early fifties—appeared from his office. "Holly! I'm so happy to see that you weren't harmed," he told her. "I want you to know that as Jimmy's widow, you're still one of us and we take an offense against one of our own very seriously. How did you get away from Officer Michaels?"

"I didn't. I was never a prisoner. Chief, there has been a terrible mistake made here. *Mason Webber* accosted me in the parking lot as I was leaving work. He pointed a gun at me and was going to kill me. He even fired it. Blake Michaels intervened. He rescued me from

Mason, and when I insisted on coming to the police, he brought me here."

He glanced around at the officers who were watching and listening. "Is that so?"

"Yes, it is. Mason Webber is the man you should be arresting. After he attacked me in the hospital parking lot, he showed up and shot at us. He's out of control."

The chief took her arm. "Perhaps we should speak privately in my office."

He led her toward a door near the back of the bullpen. Once there, he closed the door and turned to her. "I'd rather you not make such accusations in front of my officers, Holly."

"Everything I said was true. You and I both know it. Mason is out of control."

"Mason is an exemplary, longtime member of this police force. He's never been accused of erratic behavior before."

She could hardly believe her ears. Was the chief actually defending Mason? "What about what you saw in Jimmy's journal? The evidence he collected?"

"Well, the few pages you copied for me were really nothing but accusations. I looked into the incidents Jimmy mentioned and found nothing to indicate any wrongdoing. Perhaps if Jimmy had come to me instead of conducting his own inquiry, we might have some solid evidence. Or maybe there's something more substantial in the rest of the journal. You said you were going to bring it in, but you didn't."

A realization hit her and her heart sank. "It was you, wasn't it? You gave Mason those pages from Jimmy's journal." Had Blake been right that this entire force was corrupt?

There was no denying what the chief was trying to do. He wanted to paint Mason as the good guy even after he'd heard her story and seen what Jimmy had recorded. "He knew about the journal, Chief, and he had those copied pages. You're the only one I told. Did you give them to him?"

He scowled at her accusation then slid a legal pad and a pen across the desk. "Why don't you write down everything that happened, in your own words? That way, there's no discrepancy." The bite in his voice was obvious, and she knew at that moment their friendly relationship was over. His behavior didn't make him a drug trafficker like Blake was investigating, but he was certainly complicit in Mason's wrongdoings. Blake was right about the widespread corruption on this force.

She reached for the pen and pad. "I think that would be for the best."

He pushed to his feet and headed for the door. "I'll give you some time to work on that."

Holly was glad when he was gone. Her pen flew across the paper, though she was still uncertain what she would do when she finished. Given Chief Waggoner's behavior, she wasn't convinced her statement would go anywhere except the inside of the trash can.

The screech of tires outside the chief's window grabbed her attention. She put down the pad, walked to the window and saw Mason exit a car parked at the curb and hightail it toward the station. She hurried to the office door, where she could see the front of the police bullpen and Chief Waggoner speaking with another officer. He visibly tensed as Mason entered, but approached him and had words Holly couldn't hear. She held her breath as she waited. Would the chief take him into custody? Or ignore everything she'd told him? She had her answer when Mason's eyes grew wide and when Waggoner pointed toward his office. He wasn't arresting Mason or even reprimanding him.

He was handing her over to him.

Disappointment filled her. She had been wrong about Chief Waggoner. She stared around at the people in the precinct. Was there anyone here she could trust? She didn't know for sure but she knew she could trust Blake. She had to get to him.

She slipped out of the office, softly closing the door to hide her escape, and crept on tiptoe down the hall, away from the bullpen, before anyone noticed. There had to be a back door or employee entrance she could use to make her escape. She spotted an exit sign bright and beckoning at the end of the hallway and felt a rush of relief flow through her. It was her way out. The voices and footsteps heading her way stopped her from rushing toward it. She slipped into an empty office, holding her breath as two officers passed by without seeing her. Once they were out of sight, she ran to the exit and pushed open the door to freedom.

She didn't make it.

Someone grabbed her from behind, slipping his hand around her waist. "Where do you think you're going?" he snarled, his breath hot against her ear. Panic seized her as she recognized the voice.

Mason.

He pulled her into a room that appeared to be an employee break area. Her heart sank when she realized it was empty. No one around to help her or to stop Mason. She wasn't even sure anyone in this precinct would try.

He shoved her against the counter and Holly reached out, trying to stop herself. She bumped a bin and it fell, sending utensils crashing down.

"Please don't." She held out her hands to him as she'd done before. "You don't want to do this."

"Oh, no, you're wrong. I've wanted to do this for a long time."

He grabbed her again, pushed her to the floor and crawled on top of her, his hand pressing into her neck.

He was going to strangle her! Holly grabbed his hand, trying to break his grasp as fear ripped through her. She had to get away from him. She kicked and pounded on him, but he easily overpowered her. When she couldn't break his grip, she flung her hands out hoping to grab something, anything, she could use as a weapon. Her fingers locked around an object and she jammed it into Mason's neck, only then realizing it was a plastic fork. He howled but didn't loosen his grip. In fact, he tightened it, his face full of rage.

Holly gasped for breath that wouldn't come. She gripped and clawed at his hands fitfully. This couldn't be it. This couldn't be the end. *I'm not ready, God!* The room seemed to spin and fade as the lack of oxygen began to affect her. She had only moments before she lost consciousness and then her life.

But it wasn't her late husband's face she saw in the

fading light of the room. It was Blake's...hovering over Mason...a metal chair in his hands. She realized he was really there the instant he slammed the chair into the back of Mason's head.

His grip loosened and he slumped over, unconscious.

Holly quickly slid out from under him, fighting for each wonderful but excruciating breath. Blake grabbed her arm and pulled her to her feet, then slid his arm around her waist when her knees buckled.

"Are you okay?" he asked, his eyes probing.

She managed a nod and then a hoarse whisper. "What are you doing here?"

"Making sure you're okay. I can see you're not—so let's get out of here."

He kept his arm around her as they hurried through the exit. Her legs protested every step but she willed them to keep moving. They had to get away before Mason regained consciousness. Blake's truck was parked at the back and he opened the door and helped her inside before running around to the driver's side and getting in. A moment later they were speeding away.

She glanced at Blake, awestruck that he'd returned for her. He hadn't just left her—even after she'd insisted she didn't need him and had questioned his motives. He'd risked his own safety to make certain she wasn't harmed. She wasn't sure if that made him just plain dumb or incredibly kind.

"How did you know I needed help?" she asked, each syllable painful to speak.

"I was watching. I knew you were in trouble when I saw Mason pull up."

She nodded. "Chief Waggoner tried to defend Mason to me. I can't believe the chief is dirty."

Blake's jaw clenched and his fingers tightened around the steering wheel. "I should have known."

"You were right. We can't trust anyone on the police force." She reached out and placed her hand on his arm. "I'm sorry I doubted you."

"I can understand why you did. Even I would think I was paranoid if I wasn't living it. But now we *really* have to get out of town."

"How are we going to do that with the roads blocked? The police are searching for you. Mason told everyone you kidnapped me."

He turned those blue eyes on her and comfort washed through her. "We're going to find another way out of this town. I promise."

This time, she didn't doubt him.

He had no idea what their next move was. He'd walked into this, but she hadn't—Mason had dragged her in. She had to be terrified.

He shuddered, remembering the image of Mason choking her. His heart had stopped and he hadn't even thought—he'd only reacted. He wouldn't allow Mason to harm her.

She slumped in her seat, her green eyes wide with fear and her hand stroking the bruises forming on her neck. She was counting on him to keep her safe and he wouldn't let her down.

The situation looks dire, Lord, but I know nothing is impossible for You. We need a way out of this town.

They passed by a convenience store and he slowed, scoping the area. Only two cars were present in the lot—one at the gas pumps and the other parked at the front entrance. Neither was a cop car, so that was good. He was taking a risk even stopping, but they had a need they couldn't do without any longer. He had to contact Matt and the only way to do that was to find a phone.

Holly popped up in her seat as he turned the Dodge toward the gas station. "What are we doing?" she asked, her voice raw and scratchy.

"I need a phone to contact my friend. This store will have a prepaid one we can purchase."

He pulled into a parking space then cut the engine and started to pull the door handle. Her hand on his arm stopped him. It sent chills rattling through him. "I should go."

"That's not a good idea. You were barely able to stand when I pulled you from the precinct."

"I'm better now that I've gotten some oxygen to my muscles. Besides, you're too high-profile. If they've blocked the roads, they could be searching for us. I'll be right inside. You can even see me through the windows and come in if something goes wrong."

Still, he hesitated. He should be the one to go.

She blew out a weary breath. "Do you think I'm going to call the police on you?"

"No, that's not what I'm concerned about. I'm worried about your safety."

Her face softened and she smiled. "We're in this together, Blake. We have to be able to count on one another and that means you have to trust me. I'll be fine.

Only, the longer we sit here, the more obvious we become."

He knew she was right. He was the one with the gun. He needed to watch out for Mason or other officers that might spot them. He nodded his agreement and she removed her hand. He found he missed it when it was gone. He pulled out his wallet and counted several bills. "Make sure you get one that has internet access, as well. We might need it. Maybe we can find another exit on a map of the town."

She nodded and closed her hand over the cash.

"And be careful," he insisted.

She nodded then slipped out of the vehicle.

He shook off the feeling of paranoia that threatened his thoughts. If she'd wanted him captured, she could have shouted out at the police station. He hadn't forced her to come with him, but she had. And she'd been right when she'd said they needed to trust one another. The problem was he didn't trust her, and it had nothing to do with anything except her gender. He'd been fooled before by a beautiful face. He pushed away those fears. He wasn't starting a romantic relationship with her, just trying to get out of a difficult situation alive. He had to trust her and she had to trust him. Neither of them had anyone else at the moment.

He watched her move through the store, stopping every few minutes to toss something into her basket. She moved smoothly and determinedly, not like someone on the run and frightened. She put on a good act. He knew she was frightened. He'd seen her hands shaking after Mason had attacked her. She wasn't downplaying the danger they were in. She simply wasn't allowing it to control her. Amazing. He imagined her job as a nurse had trained her to stay calm in a crisis situation. That would definitely work in their favor today.

He started the engine as she exited the store and slid into the passenger's seat. "Any trouble?"

"Nope." She held out a baseball cap. "I got this for you. I thought you might need it since most of the police force knows your face. It won't hide you completely, but if you wear it low, it might shade your face a little."

"That's a good idea. Thank you." He slid the cap onto his head and pulled it low.

She nodded approvingly, then pulled out a Twizzlers and bit into it before offering him one.

"Candy?" he asked, and she shrugged.

"I eat when I'm nervous." She pulled out the phone she'd purchased to set it up as he drove, plugging it into the outlet to charge. "I had the cashier activate it for me on his cell after he explained that you had to activate it from another phone. I told him if I had another phone, I wouldn't be buying this one." She pulled up the maps on the browser and her face fell. "We were right. The bridge and the access road are the only two routes out of town. If there are any others, they're not on this map."

He looked over her shoulder at the phone, noticing the sweet scent of her hair and how soft it was as it tickled his cheek. He moved a bit so it was no longer touching him. He couldn't go there, couldn't even think it. Falling for this woman wasn't an option, so it was better not to tempt fate.

He took the phone from her and dialed Matt's cell number, thankful when he heard his voice on the line.

"I'm in trouble," he said when Matt answered. "My cover's been blown."

"What happened?" Matt's voice was serious.

"I'm not sure. Mason Webber had my file." He glanced at Holly then lowered his voice. "My *real* file, Matt. How did that happen? I thought the DOJ buried it."

"I'm not sure, but I'll find out. What's your status?"

"He shot me. Don't worry, it's just a graze. But we're on the run."

"We?"

"I'm with a woman. Holly Mathis, a nurse at the med center. She's the widow of Mason's old partner. He attacked her, too. He said he was going to set it up to look like I was obsessed with her, killed her and then killed myself. He also claimed the boss was someone high up in the town. He said they had the coroner under their control."

"But he didn't give you a name?"

"No, but when Holly went to the police, Chief Waggoner tried to hand her over to Mason. He's definitely dirty."

"We'll figure this out once you're both safe. Where are you?"

"A convenience store on the south side of town."

"Wait, you're still in Northshore? You've got to get out of there."

"We tried. All the roads are blocked. Mason has had me labeled as a dirty cop and told everyone at the precinct I kidnapped Holly. The whole force is out there looking for me."

"Let me make some calls," Matt said. "Don't worry. We'll figure this out. You just stay safe."

Blake turned to look at Holly and realized he was now responsible for keeping them both alive and well. He hoped he was up to the task. "I'll do my best," he told Matt before he pressed the off key. "We need to find a place to hide while we think this out."

"Should we go back to my friend's apartment now that Mason is gone?"

"No, he may still be watching it. We can't go to my place or yours, either." He leaned back in his seat and sighed. His mind spun at the notion of making a wrong decision. The calm he saw in her eyes meant she was depending on him.

He wouldn't let her down.

"I know a place where we can lay low for a while. It's not a great option, but it's secure." He pulled onto the road and headed west. He knew this place from his patrols. It was seedy and run-down, but hopefully it would be a safe haven for them at least for a little while until they figured out how to make their escape.

THREE

Blake drove into a part of town Holly knew by reputation only. Jimmy had always warned her against crossing over into this area. It was a notorious hangout for junkies and gangs and was known to be dangerous. Tourists were steered away from this part of the lake and even the hospital paramedics shared horror stories of coming into the area to respond to emergencies.

And Blake was choosing to go here.

"What are we doing here?"

"We need a place to hide until we can figure this out." He pulled up to a seedy motel and cut the engine.

"Are we really going to stay here?"

"This places takes cash and doesn't ask questions. It's our best option right now."

He reached out to touch her arm. "Don't worry. I'll protect you. No one will bother you as long as you're with me."

His assurance did make her feel better, but it didn't prevent her apprehension as he got out of the truck and entered the office. She could see him inside, through the glass doors, handing over cash to the clerk and receiving a key.

He returned to the truck then drove around to the back of the complex. He led her into a small but neat room. It had a double bed, a dinette set and a dresser with a small television mounted to it.

The phone he'd slipped into his pocket rang and Blake answered. "Matt, what's the news?"

His expression fell. "I understand." He ended the call then grabbed the remote. "Matt said the chief is on TV." He switched on the television to breaking news coverage.

Chief Waggoner was standing at a podium and Blake's photo was in a box at the corner of the screen. "This is Officer Blake Michaels, a recent hire with the Northshore PD. We're sad to report that we believe Officer Michaels to be a threat to our town. We're currently investigating his wrongdoings and will update more on that later, but what we do know is that he assaulted a fellow officer as he attempted to prevent Michaels from abducting a female nurse at the medical center early this morning. The hostage's name is not being released just yet."

Indignation rushed through her. "I can't believe he's sticking with the story that you kidnapped me." She felt her face flush in anger. If she'd had any doubts about Chief Waggoner, they were all gone now. She steamed, thinking about all the times since Jimmy died that he'd acted like her friend. When she'd showed him the papers from the journal, she'd thought he'd been upset to learn Jimmy had uncovered corruption in the department, but now she wondered differently. Every conversation she'd had with him took on new meaning. Had he spent the past months pressing her for information about what Jimmy might have told her? How had she mistaken the questions with just being kind?

Blake seemed unsurprised by the development. She realized he'd been right all along. He'd known how they would spin this. He'd tried to warn her—and she hadn't believed him. No, she had to be honest with herself. She had believed him. She just hadn't *wanted* to believe him. She'd been so consumed with protecting herself from more heartache and grief that she'd fooled herself into wishful thinking. She'd suspected the truth about the Northshore PD ever since finding that journal. So far she'd only read the passages about Mason, but she'd scanned the rest and knew other officers were mentioned in it. She'd known her husband was investigating dirty cops. She just hadn't wanted to believe it went as high as the chief of police.

In the midst of her struggle with Mason, she recalled she'd cried out to God. She blamed Him for this mess. He'd allowed all this to happen. He was the one who'd taken her husband from her and made her a widow at twenty-seven. Now He'd brought Mason Webber into her life.

She shuddered. "I can't believe this. Your own police department just labeled you a kidnapper. What do we do now?"

"We wait. My friends will take care of this. They'll find us a way out of town."

His friends. She'd heard him reference the DOJ in the car when he was speaking to his friend Matt. He'd told her about the drug trafficking and corruption investigations. Had he contacted the DOJ for backup? She folded her arms and locked eyes with him. "I think it's time you told me exactly what's going on. Who do you keep calling? And what does the DOJ have to do with it?"

He pushed his hand through his dark hair and sighed. "I've been working undercover for the past nine months as part of a joint task force between the DEA and DOJ. Somehow, Mason found out who I really was."

She was stunned by his revelation. He wasn't just a small-town cop investigating his fellow officers. He was a federal agent, a plant, someone who had voluntarily put himself into this position. She turned away, thinking of Jimmy and instinctively knowing he would have liked Blake. They both had the trait of jumping into the fire in the name of justice.

He knelt beside her, his expression one of compassion, and he squeezed her hands in a comforting manner. "I'm sorry you got pulled into this, Holly. I really am, but we're not alone in this. Matt and the agencies will come through for us. We have people on our side and, most importantly, we have the Lord with us."

She stared into his eyes and her heart clenched. He really believed that. She had believed it once, too, but now she figured God had forsaken her. She could put her trust in Blake Michaels to keep her safe, but she wasn't ready to put her faith back in God to do anything for her.

Blake walked to the vending machine and slipped in a handful of coins. It wasn't a real meal, but it would have to do for now until he could figure out a plan. Holly was depending on him for answers and he didn't have any. He'd heard the concern in Matt's voice. They were in real trouble. If the corruption went to the highest levels in town, they might have to fight to protect themselves.

The hairs on his neck prickled and he sensed someone watching him. He glanced around, spotting a figure on an outside balcony. Discouragement bit at him. He recognized the man as a local drug dealer. And he would no doubt report Blake's presence at the motel to Mason. They couldn't remain here.

He walked back into the room. When he'd left her, she'd seemed in a daze. Now she was pacing, determination locked into her expression.

"We can't stay here," he told her. "We have to leave now."

"What happened?"

"Someone spotted us. I'm sure he's on the phone to Mason as we speak. We should go now."

She went with him to the car without further questioning, but once inside, she said, "Tell me about the drug trafficking."

She had a right to know everything since her life was tied into his now. "There's this drug called Trixie. It's extremely dangerous and the manufacture and distribution operation is massive. My friend Matt busted up a ring in Tennessee last year but it was only part of a bigger organization. The DEA has been working with the DOJ to try to find the manufacturing facility and they believe it's right here in Northshore. I was tasked with infiltrating the department to try to find it."

"Don't the DOJ or DEA have some other way of ascertaining where this drug den is? Surely they have access to satellite imaging. Why don't they just bust it?"

"They've gotten some good leads, but they've been burned several times—getting close only to have the labs pack up and move. It's courtesy for the Feds to alert local law enforcement before they execute a raid. After a few times, they started to suspect police involvement. That's when they partnered with the DOJ."

"I don't understand. Which agency do you work for?"

"Neither."

"Then how did you get roped into taking this job?"

He shrugged. "I was in a place in my life where I needed a change. I used to be sheriff of my hometown. It was right about the time I was ready for a change that Matt approached me about this task force. They needed someone to go into the precinct, someone with certain characteristics that might lead to an invitation into corruption." He didn't tell her about the betrayal he'd suffered or Miranda's death. That was too much detail and he wasn't ready to delve into it with anyone.

"So your friend thought you were believable as a dirty cop? Either he's not a great friend, or there's something you're not telling me about your time as a sheriff."

"Something did happen, but it had nothing to do with my job as a police officer. However, Matt thought I could use it to infiltrate this group."

She gave him a wry smile. "Nice friends."

"No, he's a good friend. He knew I needed something else to focus on besides what was going on in my life."

"Look," Holly said, "we should start with figuring out who we can trust. Sometimes in nursing if there's a problem, it takes someone else to look at it to see what's happening. A new perspective, if you will."

He nodded. "I agree we need help. Was there anyone specific on the force that Jimmy trusted?"

"I'm not sure. You've been there for the past nine months. Isn't there anyone in the police department that you trust?"

He pulled his hands through his hair. He'd thought Waggoner was a stand-up guy and he'd been wrong. But he had to start thinking differently. He'd gone in looking to bond with the troublemakers. He'd made it his mission and he'd rubbed some people the wrong way in doing so. Maybe he should focus instead on those on the force who hadn't approved of his choice of friends.

One name rose to the surface. He didn't know if he could trust Gabriel or not, but Holly was right. They couldn't wait around to be either captured or rescued. They had to do something—and it could be something dangerous.

Blake drove past Gabriel Butler's house. Everything seemed quiet on the street and Holly noticed a car in the driveway. The lights were on inside the house, too, so he was definitely home. But would he help them? And could they trust him?

Blake parked several houses down and they got out. She jumped when he drew his gun. It stunned her and somehow made this all the more real. She nodded to let him know she was okay then followed him toward the house.

"Should I knock?" Holly asked when they reached the front door. "He might not recognize me right away."

He nodded then moved out of view of the peephole. She rapped on the door and listened as footsteps approached. Her gut told her someone was behind that door staring at her through the peephole. She held her breath in anticipation. Would he even open the door for her?

Seconds later she heard the lock click and the door opened. Blake pushed her aside then stepped in front of her. He raised his gun to the stunned man's head.

"There's no cash in the house," Gabriel said, coolly looking at them both as if they were common criminals.

"We're not looking for money," Blake said, pushing him back inside. Holly followed, closed the door behind them and turned the latch. "Do you know who I am?"

Gabriel stared at him then nodded slowly. "Blake Michaels. You're NPD's most wanted today." He slowly lowered his hands. "What do you two want with me?"

"I'm not here to hurt you, Gabriel. I just want to talk." To prove his intention, Blake lowered the gun and tucked it into his waistband.

Gabriel's color began to return. "I'm not sure what we have to talk about."

"Whatever you've heard about me over the radio is a lie. I didn't kidnap anyone."

"It's true," Holly said from behind him. "Mason

Webber tried to kill me. Blake interceded. He saved my life."

Gabriel glanced at her then back at Blake, and nodded. "Mason, huh? Can't say I'm surprised."

"I heard a rumor that you're upset about the corruption in the department. That's why I came to you. I'm undercover, working as part of a joint operation between the DEA and Department of Justice. I was sent here to ferret out the corruption and determine how high it goes and how it connects to the drug manufacturing ring operating out of Northshore."

Gabriel sighed then moved toward the sink in the kitchen. He poured himself a glass of water and Holly noticed his hands shaking, no doubt from the adrenaline of having a gun shoved in his face.

"I'm sorry about all this," Blake said, obviously noticing it, too. "I didn't mean to frighten you."

Gabriel gave a small laugh. "I'll admit when I saw you I thought they'd finally sent someone to kill me."

"They? Do you know who is in charge of the operation?"

"No, I don't."

"Will you help us?" Holly asked him. "We need to get out of town but all the roads are blocked."

He nodded and set down his glass. "They've got the town locked down looking for you." He glanced at Holly. "You're Jim Mathis's wife, aren't you? He was a good cop."

"Thank you for saying that," Holly said, her heart warming at the memory of Jimmy.

"Why is Mason after you?" he asked Holly.

"I thought he was obsessed with me, but now I believe he found out my husband was investigating him and was only trying to find out if Jimmy had told me anything about him. I guess he's decided it doesn't matter and he's trying to cut his losses. I should have filed charges against him for harassment months ago, but I'd hoped it would go away on its own." She sighed and glanced at Blake. "Now I know it wouldn't have done any good anyway. Chief Waggoner is just as dirty as Mason."

Gabriel's eyes widened. "The chief?" He shook his head as if absorbing the new information. "I should have known. That's why none of the reports of Mason's activities ever brought any consequences." He sighed and looked at Blake. "How do I know you're not feeding me a line? How can I believe you?"

Blake handed him a card. "Call this number and ask for Matt Ross. He's my DEA contact. He'll fill you in on the investigation."

Gabriel glanced at it then reached for his phone and stepped out of earshot to make the call.

Holly watched Blake wearing a circle in the old shag rug, but she was feeling optimistic. She touched his arm, wanting to reassure him. "I think this was a good call. He seems like a decent guy."

"Hopefully, he can help us." He placed his hand over hers and she felt a spark of electricity. She glanced up to see if he'd noticed it, too, and found his blue eyes gazing longingly at her. "I'm sorry I got you into this," he said, his voice low and deep.

She shuddered at the timbre of it but rushed to reassure him.

"You didn't. You saved my life today. Twice." She felt the sudden urge to fling herself into his arms and find comfort in his embrace. But she tamped down that feeling and took a step away from him, breaking the connection. She had to remain on alert and that meant reigning in her emotions, especially in front of someone she was depending on to get her through this.

Gabriel reappeared from the kitchen. "You checked out. How can I help you?"

"We need to get out of town. Any suggestions?"

"Well, the roads may be blocked, but you could go across the lake. I have a boat docked at the marina. They might not be able to monitor the entire lake."

Blake glanced at her and Holly nodded. That was the best idea she'd heard in a while and hope bubbled anew. "We'll try that."

Gabriel removed a set of keys from a hook by the door. "It's at the Bridge Bay Marina, slip eighteen. I'll drive you."

"That's not necessary," Blake said.

But Gabriel wouldn't hear of it. "I insist. I want to make certain you make it out of town safely. I've been working secretly with Mayor Banks to try to clean up the force. We had no idea the Feds were already involved. It's good to have someone else on the side of justice."

They loaded into his SUV and headed toward the lake.

Holly sat back and found herself praying they would make it. It was still her instinct to go to God with her troubles, but she wouldn't allow herself to. God had let her down too many times. She had only Blake to depend on now.

Gabriel turned into the marina and cut the engine.

Blake pulled out his gun and reached for the door handle. "Let me check it out first to make sure the coast is clear."

He got out and disappeared down the pier. Holly watched him anxiously. Her nerves were on edge, but with a hopeful excitement for a change. If they were able to reach the boat and make it across the lake, she might finally be able to put this nightmare behind her. She wished she had Jimmy's journal with her to hand over to Blake. She could trust him with it now. He could pass it along to his DEA friend and perhaps some good would come from Jimmy's final investigation. She smiled, liking the thought that he was still reaching out, still helping the fight for justice, even from the grave.

"You're smiling," Gabriel said. "Something funny?"

"No, nothing. I was just thinking that a few hours ago, I didn't even know Blake. Now, I'm ready to hand over my husband's last possession."

"His possession?"

"A few days ago, I found a journal Jimmy had been writing about corruption he suspected Mason was involved in. He was investigating the drug ring."

Gabriel let out a long breath. "I had no idea. Do you think that's what got him killed?"

A shiver ran through her. She hadn't let that suspicion become a conscious thought since finding the journal. "I don't know," she rasped, choking on the emotion that suddenly overtook her.

He seemed to have noticed he'd upset her. "I found the circumstances of his death suspicious, but I haven't looked into his case. I shouldn't have said anything. That was insensitive of me."

"No, it's fine. I know now that Mason is capable of murder. Until a few days ago, I trusted what the police told me about Jimmy's death. Now I just don't know what to believe."

Blake reappeared at the window. "Everything seems clear. Let's go."

They got out and headed down the dock until they reached slip eighteen. Gabriel tossed Blake the keys then bent to untie the boat as Blake and Holly climbed aboard.

Pounding footsteps on the dock grabbed Holly's attention. She turned to see Mason running toward them. Terror ripped through her. "He's here!" she cried, causing Blake to turn.

"Watch out!" he shouted.

Gabriel stood and turned just as Mason raised his gun and fired. Holly screamed again as Gabriel slumped over then fell off the dock and into the water.

"Start the boat!" Blake hollered as he leaped over the edge of the boat onto the dock. He pulled his gun and fired as Mason ducked for cover. He knew he needed to get Holly to safety, but he couldn't leave Gabriel to Mason's hands. He peered into the black water where Gabriel had fallen, but saw nothing. He would have surfaced if he could have. Given the way he'd slumped when Mason had shot him, Blake doubted he'd even been alive when he hit the water.

The roar of the boat's engine was music to his ears, but before he could get back to Holly, Mason tackled him from seemingly out of nowhere. They hit the dock together and the gun slipped from Blake's hand. He grappled for it but couldn't reach it before Mason grabbed him and tried to wrangle him into a choke hold.

He sneered as Blake struggled to break the hold.

"You're dead!" he snapped. "I will rip your heart out."

"You…don't…have…to do this, Mason." Blake's words came out in spurts as he struggled to keep conscious against Mason's grip.

He snorted. "The last man who threatened me had an unfortunate accident while responding to a burglary call. And I liked him better than I like you."

Blake was stunned. Was he talking about Holly's husband? Holly had said he'd died in the line of duty. If Mason was telling the truth, Holly would be devastated.

Suddenly he heard the clank of something hard and felt Mason's grip loosen. Blake pulled away and saw Holly swing a crowbar at Mason's head. It hit him hard for a second time and the man went down.

Blake grabbed her hand then his gun and ran back to the boat. They had to get out of there, and now.

Mason crawled to his feet and started firing wildly as Blake and Holly dove onto the boat. Blake rolled to the console, shifted into gear and opened up the engine, glancing back to be sure Holly stayed down. She was thankfully hugging the deck of the boat as they roared away.

From the dock, he could hear Mason hollering after them.

When they were out of range, Holly looked up at

Blake, her own turmoil-filled emotions shining in her green eyes. "He killed Gabriel," she said.

Blake nodded. His jaw clenched hard but he ducked his head to hide his rage. It wasn't right that Mason could wreak such havoc on other people's lives.

His mind retreated to the men he'd lost in battle in Afghanistan. He didn't know Gabriel as well, but they'd both been fighting on the same side. "I know."

Holly stood and leaned against him, wrapping her arms protectively around him. He stiffened at first, till he felt her pounding heart and her ragged breath echoing his own. He relaxed, and returned the embrace as best he could while steering the boat. It felt right, even though he wasn't sure if she was trying to reassure him or to comfort herself. It didn't matter. He supposed they both needed it now.

"Thank you, Holly," he whispered, surprised to find his voice choked with emotion. He tried to concentrate on driving the boat, but she wasn't going to let it go.

"Have you lost people before?" she asked him.

His whole body tensed at her question. The sway of the boat and the dark night provided good cover. He'd lost too many people. "Before I was a cop, I was an Army Ranger. One night, my team was ambushed. All but six of us were killed."

"Oh, Blake, I'm so sorry."

"It was a while ago, but it still hurts." He paused a beat. "Then last year…" He hesitated. She didn't really need to know the awful details of Miranda's death, but something inside him wanted him to share with her the loss he'd felt. "My fiancée was murdered."

She gasped and tightened her arms around him. "I'm so sorry, Blake. I know how terrible that kind of loss is."

It was true she knew about losing someone she loved and, if Mason was to be believed—and Blake did believe him—her husband had also been murdered by a madman.

A distant, low buzz grabbed his attention. His head jerked in the direction of the choppy noise—growing louder each second—and he scanned the dark water. He adjusted his direction and tried to coax more speed out of the older vessel, but he soon spotted a light headed their way. Another boat.

Suddenly a spotlight flickered on and he identified the sound of a speedboat engine gaining on them with each second.

"It's him," Holly cried, and Blake knew she was right. And he wasn't alone. Several others had joined him.

"Take the wheel," he said, pulling the gun from his belt. "Keep going as fast as possible."

"Can we outrun them?"

Shots rang out and hit the boat.

"Get down!" Blake screamed, pulling her to the floor. The approaching vessel sped up, coming straight at them. He braced himself for the impact. It rammed them and tossed the boat. He reached for her hand then grabbed for something to hold on to as the boat arched and nearly capsized. For several, horrifying seconds, he envisioned them going over.

Then, suddenly, capsizing wasn't their biggest problem. Mason lit something on fire and tossed it over. It landed only inches from Holly. Blake smelled gasoline and knew Mason meant to burn them up.

"We can't stay here," Blake told her. "Our only hope is in the water."

She nodded and he helped her slip over the side. Blake slid in beside her and grabbed her hand. "Stay close. We can't get separated."

"Which way is the shore?" she asked, scanning the horizon. "Can we make it to the other side?"

He shook his head. "No, it's too far. We'll never make it. We need to head back to the town shore. It's that direction." He motioned then pushed off and began swimming. He heard the water rustling beside him and knew she was keeping up just fine. The roar of the engines and the colliding of the two boats had made the water rough and choppy. He stopped and glanced back. Gabriel's boat was now ablaze and those on the other boat were searching the water with the spotlight.

"Don't stop!" Blake told her, pressing her to continue. "We have to keep going."

She reached the bank first and climbed up, grabbing hold of a low-hanging branch to pull herself out of the water. Blake was right behind her, crawling onto solid ground. Gratitude rushed through him that they'd made it safely to shore, but he knew their journey hadn't ended. They were still trapped in Northshore and on the run.

He stood and looked back at Gabriel's boat, which was already low in the water. Mason and his men were shouting at one another and their voices lifted across the waves. They were searching for them.

Blake grabbed her arm. "We should get out of here. It won't take them long to figure out where we are."

She nodded and followed him, but she was soaking wet and the Arkansas night was unusually chilly. She shivered and Blake slipped his arm around her for warmth. They needed to go somewhere they could get dry and warm.

Holly was tense beside him. He felt the energy flowing off her in waves. His instinct was to reach out for another embrace—pull her into his arms and reassure her that everything would be fine. He surprised himself. He hardly knew this woman. Why was he having thoughts like this? So he was stunned when she leaned into him for warmth and he had to wrap his arms around her and pull her close.

"Where are we going?" she asked him.

He had an idea of someone else they could turn to for help. "We need to find a place to lay low for a while and dry off."

"It won't be easy. Two people, soaking wet, traipsing through town? We're bound to draw looks."

They would have to be extra careful. They had no vehicle and now Mason had just upped everything by strongly implying he had killed a fellow police officer. When Blake had seen Gabriel slump forward and fall into the water, horror had rippled through him—Mason was a murderer and he was surely going to find them and attempt to finish what he'd started.

FOUR

Holly shivered from the chill in the night. She was soaked through and through. She leaned into Blake's large frame, thankful for his arms blocking the wind. They'd left Blake's vehicle back at Gabriel's house and the police had surely towed it by now. She didn't know what they were going to do. All she could do was trust Blake.

He tightened his hold around her and she sank into the comfort of his arms, astonished by the way her pulse quickened at the masculine scent of him. *Stop it.* She was just being foolish. She was cold, wet and terrified—of course she would find comfort in the arms of a strong, protective soul.

She couldn't trust her emotions. She hadn't had such thoughts about any man except Jimmy since they'd fallen in love. Even when her friends had encouraged her to get out and start dating again, she'd refused. The desire to meet someone and fall in love again had been the last thing on her mind. So she was surprised by the intensity of her feelings toward Blake.

He led her stealthily toward town, avoiding populated areas and watching out for cars passing by. Once, he pulled her down so fast into a ditch that her arm was still sore. She rubbed it and tried not to complain. *When you're running for your life, you don't worry about minor inconveniences and troublesome aches.* She was fortunate to have Blake with her. Where would she be without him? She knew the answer. She would be dead in the parking lot of Northshore Medical Center.

He stopped and crouched behind a row of bushes, looking into the town square. "We'll never make it anywhere on foot. We have to steal a car."

"Steal a car?" Holly gasped.

His face flushed. "Borrow a car. I don't like it, either, but we have little choice. We have to get somewhere safe and dry before the police spot us."

"Have you ever stolen—er, borrowed—a car before?"

He shot her a glance that answered and silenced her. "I wasn't always a cop," he told her then scanned the area. "I'm going to go check out that pickup parked at the curb. Keep a lookout, but when I wave to you, come running and get inside."

She nodded and looked around. Her hands were shaking from the cold. She hated the thought of stealing someone else's car, but Blake was right. Mason had left them little choice and, surely, if the owner knew the circumstances, he would understand.

What would she do if she did spot someone approaching? Panic shot through her. Blake had left her to watch, but she had no idea how to alert him. Should she whistle or do a birdcall like she'd seen on television? She needed the "Survivor's Guide to Running for Your Life." She grinned as she realized Blake could easily write it. *I'm so tired, I'm loopy.*

Thankfully the only people she spotted were across the square, gathered outside the coffee shop, talking. They weren't looking this way and no one else seemed out and about. She checked again then let her gaze settle on Blake, who was already inside the pickup.

He motioned for her and when the engine started up, she felt relieved as well as a little impressed. Then she remembered where he'd gotten his practice and decided God must have used that time in his life to prepare him for this. As thin as that reasoning was, it made her feel better.

She slid into the passenger's seat and he roared off nearly before her door was closed.

"No one saw us," she told him.

"I know. It was a clean getaway."

He seemed pleased with himself—which rubbed her the wrong way—but when he cranked up the heater, she forgot everything except warming up. She held her hands in front of the vents and sank into the warmth of the air.

"Rub your hands together. It creates friction, which warms them faster. And check in the back seat. Maybe there's a blanket, or jacket, or something you can use to get warm."

She reached over the back of the seat and found a pair of gloves and an Arkansas Razorbacks fleece blanket.

She felt fortunate to find that considering they were at the back end of summer.

He nodded. "You wrap up in the blanket."

She saw him shiver and knew he was cold, too. "We'll share it."

She sat beside him on the bench seat and pulled the blanket over them both. It wasn't a large blanket so she scooted closer to him and draped it over them both, allowing his arms to poke out so he could drive.

"It should be warming up in here soon," he said with just a hint of hesitation in his voice. Did it bother him to have her so close? "What we need to do is get into some dry clothes," he continued.

"Let's go to my house," she suggested. "I still have some of Jimmy's clothes and I'm sure they'll fit you. We can both get dry."

"That's not a good idea. Mason may have it staked out."

"Or maybe he's moved on already. It doesn't hurt to try. Besides, we can park in my neighbor's driveway on the next street over and cut through the backyard. They've gone out of town to visit their daughter for two weeks. If someone is watching the house, they'll be watching the front. Besides, we have to go somewhere. We'll be careful."

He seemed to consider this for a moment then nodded his reluctant agreement.

She gave him directions and sat back as he drove, suddenly settling into a comfortable silence. As the pickup warmed up, and so did they, he seemed to relax. His hands loosened their grip on the steering wheel and his jaw eased. Holly was surprised by the way her skin prickled at being so close to him. The air in the cab warmed and her heart started beating a little faster at sitting right next to him. She wanted to know more about this man in whose hands she'd placed her life.

"So, you were a car thief, were you?" Her tone was light and teasing and the sly smile he gave her told her he knew she was only curious.

"In a manner of speaking. Part of my duties as an Army Ranger, along with my fellow Ranger, Garrett, was to disable any vehicles that could be used by the enemy to escape or chase us during a strike. Garrett was the one with the experience. When he was a teenager in foster care, he fell in with a crime ring that used to steal cars. Thankfully, the Army cleaned up his ways. He taught me everything I know about borrowing cars."

She felt her face redden. She'd thought he'd been a car thief and he'd actually only been serving his country and protecting his Ranger squad. "Thank Garrett for me the next time you talk to him," she said teasingly. "We'd still be icicles on the side of the road if it wasn't for him schooling you."

He grinned. "I'll do that." He turned on the blinker as he approached her subdivision and all the lightheartedness flowed out of him. His jaw clenched again and his shoulders squared as he prepared for a possible confrontation. "Maybe you should get down out of sight. I want to sweep around the block to see if there's any surveillance on the house."

She slid onto the floorboard and wrapped the fleece around her. She couldn't see outside, but she could see

Blake's face as his gaze moved, seeking anything out of place. She was impressed with this man in a manner that surprised her. For a few moments there he'd felt more like a longtime friend than a near stranger. She liked the way his mouth had curved into a grin and his face had lightened for a moment.

But she'd also learned he was ex-military. Being a cop was dangerous enough, but he was used to taking risks in his duties as an Army Ranger and the last thing she needed in her life was to lose someone else. She couldn't let her heart go there with Blake—no matter how drawn she was to him.

He turned into her neighbor's driveway and put the pickup into Park. "I didn't see anybody, but better safe than sorry. We'll cut through the yard."

She led the way but Blake remained close behind her, his gun drawn and ready for action. He'd also borrowed a rifle from the back window of the pickup.

She opened the gate to the backyard and walked to the back door. She usually kept it locked, but she doubted a lock would have stopped Blake or Mason from getting inside. She needn't have bothered. The glass in her back window frame was broken and a peek inside showed the house had been ransacked.

Blake pushed open the door and rushed past her, gun raised as he searched the house for intruders.

Holly stood in the dining room and saw her grandmother's china smashed against the floor. She gave in to the tears at the pure malicious intent—it wasn't valuable, but Mason knew how much the china meant to her. They'd talked about it one evening when Mason had eaten dinner with them.

She stepped through the shards crunching beneath her feet and stared at her living room. It, too, was destroyed, the couch cushions cut open and stuffing covering the floor. Her framed family photos were broken and her television stand in pieces. The TV was on the floor, the screen shattered.

Blake entered, putting away his weapon. "No one is here. They must have been looking for something. Any clue what it was?"

Jimmy's journal.

"I have a pretty good idea."

She walked into the bedroom and opened her closet. Most of her belongings were also strewn about. She held her breath, wondering if Mason had found the secret compartment and already retrieved the journal. Relief flooded her when she saw that the wood was untouched. They hadn't known about the secret compartment—and hadn't stumbled across it as they'd ripped her home to shreds.

She pushed at the wall and the piece popped out.

Blake sucked in an audible breath. "A nice little hiding place. Very cool."

"I found it a few days ago. I was finally packing up Jimmy's side of the closet and tripped. I hit the wall and fell. And when I did, this panel popped open." She reached inside, grateful when she felt her hand touch the familiar leather. She took it out and showed it to Blake. "This is what I found inside."

He took it and skimmed through the pages.

"It's notes about Mason and other members of the force. Jimmy was investigating crooked cops."

Blake locked eyes with Holly. "Just like me."

She nodded. "Just like you. Only, he's dead." The tremor in her voice surprised even her. She hadn't realized until just this moment how frightened she was that something might happen to Blake and she would once again be all alone, only this time with a maniac out to get her.

"May I read this?" he asked.

The request was so sincere that she actually believed he might put it back into the wall if she said no.

She nodded. "I haven't read much of it. I copied some pages when I realized what it was and showed them to Chief Waggoner."

"The chief knows about this journal?"

She nodded again and felt tears slip down her face. "I thought he was someone I could trust. The moment I discovered this journal, everything I knew about my life and my community shattered."

"What did he say?"

"He tried to shrug it off like it was nothing. He said it was notes for an investigation Jimmy had been working on. He asked me to bring him the journal and gave me some spin about Jimmy helping to end injustice even from the grave."

"Then what happened?"

"Well, Mason tried to kill me the next day—so I guess he didn't think I believed him." She sighed. "Something just didn't feel right, but I thought he was only upset about corruption on his force. I should have seen it. He was so concerned about getting his hands on that book. He even offered to drive to the house with me right then to get it. I told him I was on my way to work and was finally able to put him off for a while by telling him I would get it once my shift was over."

"You have good instincts, Holly. You should learn to trust them more."

She reached for a box and opened it, pulling out a pair of jeans and a T-shirt. "These were Jimmy's, but you're about the same size. They should fit you."

He reached for the clothes and his hand stroked hers, sending a buzz of electricity through her. It stunned her. She shouldn't be feeling these things in this house, in this room she'd shared with her husband—especially while she was handing his clothes to another man. Yet it seemed perfectly natural to have Blake there and to trust him—with not only her safety, but also with Jimmy's last thoughts.

"I'll take good care of this," he said, holding up the journal, and she believed him. He turned and walked out of the room.

Holly found some clean, dry clothes among the rubble and quickly changed. She even found an overnight bag and stuffed in a few things. When she came out, Blake was in the living room, standing at the window, keeping watch. Her heart beat a little faster at his protective stance.

Stop it, Holly. She refused to think of Blake that way. She wasn't ready to consider any man that way, but especially not a risk-taker like Blake Michaels. One look at the portrait of her and her husband was all the reminder she needed. She couldn't—she *wouldn't*—live with someone she would worry about every time he left the house.

"Maybe we should stay here," she said. "They've come and gone. They probably won't return, right?"

"Mason is smart. He knows we jumped into the water so he'll know we need to change clothes and that our options are limited. He might sweep back by here just in case."

"Well, we have time to grab a bite, don't we? I have some leftover lasagna in the refrigerator." She turned to go into the kitchen then realized the refrigerator wasn't upright. She turned back to Blake. "A little help, please?"

He righted the appliance and Holly removed a pan of lasagna that had somehow survived the tip-over. She grabbed two forks, handed him one and then poured them each a glass of iced tea.

"I hope you don't mind cold lasagna."

"Absolutely not," Blake said as he dug in. "This is good."

"Thank you. I enjoy it. Lately, I've been making way too much food. I haven't figured out this cooking-for-one thing just yet."

He gave her a sympathetic smile. "I'm sure you'll get the hang of it with time."

She nodded but suddenly felt like crying into her lasagna. "They say time heals all wounds. It's been over a year and I'm still waiting."

He lowered his head and whispered, "I know what you mean."

Her mind zeroed in on that ring she knew was in his wallet. His fiancée's? She saw the same heartache she knew so well mirrored in his expression. Yes, indeed, he knew the pain of loss.

He reached across the table and squeezed her hand and she clasped her fingers into his without hesitation, marveling that sitting in the kitchen eating cold lasagna could feel so right.

Headlights hit the front window and Blake tensed and drew his hand away. He walked to the window and peeked out.

"They're here."

Anger ripped through her, overriding any fear she felt at the moment. Couldn't she have a few minutes without Mason hunting them down? She gave a weary sigh then grabbed her bag at Blake's urging and headed for the back door. He moved behind her as she ran across the yard and through the gate.

He started the engine as she pulled the seat belt over her. The whirl of police sirens filled the air and she saw the glowing lights across the night sky as they drove away from the house she'd shared with Jimmy.

Blake gripped the steering wheel. He couldn't wait to get on with reading that journal, but he also couldn't get that moment in Holly's kitchen out of his mind. He'd felt her shiver when he'd touched her hand and he'd loved the wave of electricity that flitted up his arm. Attraction wasn't the issue. Of course he was attracted to her. She was knockout gorgeous, but he was discovering there was so much more to her than her looks.

"Where are we going now?" she asked. He saw the trust in her eyes—looking to him to provide. He could sense how much she hated leaving her home. Now he had to find another place for them to stay tonight, somewhere safe and private where he could spend a few hours reading through the journal.

"I have an idea." He picked up the burner phone and dialed the number of his pastor and friend, Dave Talbert. He hated to impose on anyone but felt certain Dave would never believe the lies Mason was spreading about him and would be quick to offer his help.

When the pastor answered, Blake explained the situation and, as expected, Dave offered them a safe place to sleep for the night.

As they pulled up to his house, Blake noticed that he'd left the garage door open. He quickly drove the stolen pickup inside, knowing the pastor would have a lot to answer for if anyone saw an unfamiliar vehicle parked outside his house. Blake had to make certain they weren't spotted.

Dave appeared in the doorway that led from the garage to the kitchen. Pressing a button on a panel on the wall, he lowered the garage door as Blake and Holly exited the pickup.

He offered his hand and Blake shook it, gratefully. "Thank you for your help," he said. "This is Holly Mathis. She's a nurse at NMC."

Dave reached out to shake Holly's hand. "It's nice to meet you, Holly. I wish it was under better circumstances."

"Me, too. Thank you for letting us stay here."

"Not a problem. I've known Blake for a while now and I know these accusations against him must be false."

"Yes, they are," she assured him. "Blake saved me. He's definitely one of the good guys."

She glanced at Blake and he felt his face redden. He wasn't used to being lauded, but it felt good to hear her say nice things about him.

"Well, let's get inside, shall we?"

He led them into the house and motioned to Holly. "The spare room is down that hall. I thought you could take it. And, Blake, you can take the couch."

"That's fine," Blake said, nodding as he led Holly down the hall to the spare room. She seemed hesitant, so he rubbed her shoulders. "It'll be fine," he assured her. "We're safe here. I trust Dave."

She ran a hand through her hair. "I'm sorry. I'm not sure who I can trust anymore." She turned to look at him and smiled. "Except for you. I trust you, Blake. If you say we're safe, then I believe you."

She suddenly stepped forward and leaned into his chest, catching him off guard. "I don't know what I would have done without you."

The scent of her hair wafted to him and his head spun with the lovely fragrance. He was suddenly unsure of what to do with his hands. Should he embrace her? Pat her shoulder? What?

Finally he placed his hand on her back and it felt so good. His voice was choked when he spoke again. "I won't let anything happen to you, Holly. We will get through this."

She stared up at him, her green eyes again searching for answers, for protection.

His heart lurched as he stroked her arm. It felt so good to be close to someone. It had been so long since he'd touched soft skin and delicate features or gazed into wide, wondering eyes looking to him to make everything better.

He took a deep, fortifying breath and removed his hands from her back. He couldn't go down that road. He'd already gotten too close to her, his mind racing with thoughts about her. She was smart and capable and somehow he'd let her wiggle in under his guard and pierce the armor he hid behind.

She stared up into his face and sighed, then pulled away. "I'm sorry. I shouldn't have done that. I've made you uncomfortable."

"No, you didn't. It's fine." He couldn't help the roar of attraction he felt for her—but had it been so obvious that she'd noticed? He hoped not. He had to keep reminding himself that love and romance were not in his future.

"I'll let you get some sleep. Don't worry. I'll be standing guard."

Once she disappeared into the bedroom, he ran his hand over his stubbly chin. This was getting way out of hand. He had to take control of this attraction he felt for her. It was downright dangerous for him to get so close.

Lord, I can't do this again.

He walked into the den and lowered himself onto the couch.

The aroma of coffee wafted through the room and

he spotted Dave standing there in the doorway holding two mugs.

Blake grinned and took the one he offered. "Thank you. And not just for the coffee."

"My pleasure." He pulled up a chair and straddled it. "Now, let's talk."

Blake took a sip of coffee then set it down. "You want to know if I did the things they're saying. I thought you said you knew me better than that?"

"This isn't about the news or even about the girl. It's about you."

"What about me?"

"I don't know, Blake. We've become friends over the past few months. We've discussed your fiancée and her betrayal. I feel like I should know you very well—only there's always been this part of you that you held back. I think it's about time you told me who you really are."

Blake rubbed his chin and picked up his coffee again. "You're right. It was never my intention to deceive you, Dave."

Dave gave him a rueful stare. "You see, when I hear a sentence that starts that way, I know I'm about to learn I've been deceived."

"I've been working undercover as part of a DEA and DOJ task force. I came to town to ferret out corruption in the police department and take down a major drug manufacturing ring."

Dave whistled and dragged his fingers through his hair. "Wow. I had no idea."

"Mason discovered what I was doing. He tried to kill me. Then he tried to kill Holly."

"Did you contact the police?"

"The force is corrupt, Dave. I don't know who I can trust there. Besides, I reached out to someone already and now he's dead."

"And what about the girl?"

"What about her? She's in trouble. I'm trying to help her."

"And that's all?"

He felt jittery and shrugged. "I can't deny she's beautiful. But she's more than that, Dave. She's also smart and capable and brave. I feel myself falling for her—but I know it could never work out between us."

"You don't trust her?"

"No, I do trust her. It's just…" He hesitated, uncertain even of his own feelings. "I suppose I'm just so used to being disappointed in people that I'm having a hard time allowing myself to let down my guard with her."

Dave shook his head then finished off his coffee. "You can't go through life always waiting for the other shoe to drop. Learn to trust in the Lord. He'll never steer you wrong."

Blake wanted to believe that, but he'd already been let down once. Could he even trust himself to hear where God was leading? He couldn't deny he was very attracted to Holly. Was that clouding his judgment?

Dave disappeared into the other room and Blake reached for the journal, intending to stretch out on the couch and read for a while, but movement in the hallway grabbed his attention and put him on full alert. He relaxed when he realized it was only Holly.

He tried to slow the beating of his heart as she entered the room, her hair rumpled from probably only a few minutes of sleep. "What's the matter? Can't sleep?"

She shook her head and moved farther into the room. Her face flushed guiltily and he realized she'd been listening to his and Dave's conversation.

"I wasn't eavesdropping," she told him. "I didn't mean to overhear."

He felt his guard go up. How much had she heard? He cringed, realizing it must have been the part about him falling for her. Or that he had doubts about her.

"I have a confession to make." She padded across the room and joined him on the couch. He watched as she tucked a strand of hair behind her ear—a nervous habit he'd noticed before. "When Mason attacked me in the parking lot and you intervened...in the truck on the way out of town when you showed me your police ID, something fell out of your wallet." She hesitated. "And so did the ring."

His eyes widened and he suddenly realized what she was talking about. Miranda's engagement ring. She'd seen it.

"Did it belong to her, your fiancée? I mean, you don't have to tell me. It's really none of my business. I guess I'm just curious about it and want to know you better."

He nodded then opened his wallet and pulled out the ring.

"She's the one who was murdered, isn't she?"

"Yes, she is."

"Like Jimmy?"

He shot her a curious glance. Did she know her husband hadn't died in the line of duty? That Mason had murdered him? She seemed to, although he wasn't sure how.

"I guess I've suspected it for a while. Something about Mason's story didn't add up and then when I found the journal…" She shuddered and Blake pulled her into his arms. She needed a strong shoulder and he could give her one. Who knew better than him what it felt like to have someone you loved killed in that way? But their stories weren't exactly the same.

"There's more to my story," he admitted. "My friend Colton took a job protecting a woman from a powerful loan shark who wanted her dead. The loan shark offered a large cash reward to anyone willing to tell him where she was hiding out. Miranda, my fiancée, wanted that reward. She kidnapped Laura, drugged her and handed her over to a man she knew would kill her."

Holly gasped. "How awful."

"Only, instead of giving her the money he'd promised, he put a bullet in her head."

Her mouth gaped open in surprise. "That's terrible. I'm so sorry, Blake. That was the incident that made your friend suggest you were ready for a change of scenery, wasn't it?"

He nodded. "I could hardly face anyone after that. I was supposed to be the law but no one respected me anymore." He sighed and tossed the ring onto the end table, where it bounced then spun a few times before settling onto the wood. "I lost everything." He rubbed a hand over his head. It was difficult reliving this, but he wanted her to know. It felt good to open up. He only hoped his sordid tale didn't frighten her away.

"When I came to Northshore, I started going to church because I thought it would be a good way to insinuate myself into the community. Instead I found myself drawn in by the Scriptures the pastor was teaching every Sunday.

"If you had asked me a year ago about my relationship with the Lord, I would have told you it was good and that I had a strong faith. But I was so wrong. I realize now I wasn't allowing the God I claimed to love to influence my life at all. I met Miranda and fell into a relationship with her without even consulting the Lord's opinion. I look back now and see all the signs I wasn't paying any attention to. I can't blame God for my wrong choices when I made them all on my own."

"Oh, Blake. I had no idea." She stared around then sighed. "And now in trying to escape one mess, you've jumped right into another."

"I guess I have, but this one is different." He touched her face and locked eyes with her to drive home his point. "One thing I don't doubt, Holly, is that I'm right where I'm supposed to be."

She stared up at him and her breath caught.

Suddenly his attraction for her flared and he was drawn to her like metal to a magnet. He touched her face, stroking her lips, and felt her quiver beneath his hand. When his lips claimed hers, she leaned into him and kissed him back. His hands found her hair and pushed through her soft, dark curls. Everything about the moment felt right, but reality hit him hard and fast and he broke away, breathing heavy. It was too fast—way too fast—and he was letting the emotion of the moment get away from him.

"I'm sorry," he whispered. "I shouldn't have done that."

"I'm not sorry," she whispered, then stood and padded back down the hall.

He fell back onto the couch, his heart pounding as much from her words as from her kiss. She wasn't sorry. She shared his attraction. His mind spun at the idea that something was happening between them. He wouldn't deny that he was attracted to her, but what he'd told her had been true. He wouldn't jump into a new relationship headfirst without knowing it was part of God's plan for his life.

Oh, Lord, guide my way.

FIVE

Blake watched Mayor Banks as she left her house the next morning and drove into town. He followed her in the old truck, Holly by his side. He hadn't figured out the best way to approach her yet. Could they trust her? Gabriel had claimed to secretly be working with her, so Blake hoped she was someone they could turn to for help. But it wasn't as if they could stroll into her office and make an appointment. Gabriel might have trusted Mayor Banks, but Blake was wary of everyone right now, especially someone he didn't know.

He'd met the mayor before in passing and had seen her in the precinct talking to Chief Waggoner. He knew the chief couldn't stand her. Considering the chief was dirty, that was a point in the mayor's favor. However, that wasn't enough for Blake to just waltz up to her and tell her about a giant conspiracy to murder him and Holly.

Holly sat beside him in the pickup. She had that trusting look in her eyes again, like a lamb on the way to the slaughter, and he again hadn't a clue how to proceed.

It didn't help that Blake had spent the previous night reading through Jimmy's journal and found several passages that indicated Jimmy had been investigating Gabriel, as well. That information made his mind spin—he didn't even know how to process it. Had he known that beforehand, he might not have even turned to Gabriel for help. But maybe Jimmy suspected him because he'd been keeping his work with the mayor a secret.

"Did you find anything in Jimmy's journal?" Holly asked, pulling him back to the present—her beautiful green eyes staring at him for answers. They hadn't spoken about what had happened last night. What had seemed so right then felt slightly awkward in the light of day. Yet her words continued to haunt him.

I'm not sorry.

He pushed those thoughts away. He had to focus on here and now. "Actually, I found a lot. A number of names I've suspected as being dirty cops also appeared in your husband's journal. Apparently he'd been investigating them, too. If I can compare our lists and look for overlapping names, it will probably give us a good indication of who we can trust on the force and who we can't."

"I'm glad it's helping. Jimmy would like that someone is using the information to do good."

He smiled at the innocent way she spoke of her husband and thought again about what Mason had told him.

He'd been trying to figure out a way to break the news to her. Finally he just decided he had to do it. She'd admitted she had suspected as much.

"Holly, do you remember last night when you were

talking about Jimmy being killed? You said you thought he was murdered by Mason?"

She nodded. "I think he knew Jimmy was investigating him."

"When Mason and I were struggling on the pier, he said something to me. He told me the last person who crossed him had an unfortunate accident. I think he was talking about Jimmy."

Pain filled her face, but she managed to keep it in check. "I wish I could say I was surprised, but I'm not."

He nodded and felt a wave of sympathy for her. She was taking the information well. Too well?

Oh, stop it. She's only trying to hold on so she doesn't fall apart.

He parked the truck a few rows down from where the mayor had parked. Holly pointed out the window at the woman approaching the coffee shop. "There she is."

He pulled his gun, checked it then scanned the area around the coffee shop. "We still need to figure out the best way to approach her."

"I'll do it as she's leaving the coffee shop."

He saw Mayor Banks make her way toward the coffee shop, stopping a few times to speak with people on the street. Holly was right. She would blend in with the others better than he would. Everyone appeared to be in the morning rush, and no one was giving the others on the street more than a passing glance.

She pulled her hair into a bun then donned a pair of sunglasses she'd found in the glove compartment. "I'll be right back."

He wanted to stop her, pull her back inside—but they

needed this connection with Mayor Banks. "Be careful," he said instead. He wanted to get out and shadow her, but he saw no place to hide. Sitting in the pickup was the best choice.

Lord, please keep her safe.

She blended into the crowd and looked like just another woman hurrying along. She turned to give a quick glance back before opening the shop door and disappearing inside.

Holly took a deep breath as she entered. The aroma of coffee and muffins filled the room and people milled around, standing in line waiting or sitting at tables. She stepped in behind Mayor Banks. The woman was older with short dark hair and a conservative suit dress and heels. Although Holly had tried to put on a brave face in front of Blake, she didn't know how to handle this. What if the mayor turned her in? Or was working with Mason, Chief Waggoner and whoever else they were in cahoots with?

She reached out and tapped the woman's shoulder before she lost her nerve and let fear wrap her in knots. The mayor turned around and gave her a smile. "Good morning," she said.

Holly responded similarly, adding, "I was hoping to speak with you privately."

She reached for a business card and handed it to Holly. "My office is always open to the public. If you call this number, my assistant can tell you when I have an available appointment."

"No," Holly persisted. "This is important. We can't wait for an appointment."

The mayor glanced around again and her smile faded. "We?"

"My name is Holly Mathis." She leaned closer and whispered, "One of the local police officers tried to kill me yesterday and we don't know who we can trust. We went to Gabriel Butler for help last night. He said he was working with you to uncover corruption in the police department."

Mayor Banks lowered her head, grabbed Holly's arm and pulled her to the side. Her voice was low and concerned. "Gabriel told you about that?"

Holly nodded. "He was trying to help us—but they killed him."

Her eyes widened in shock. "Gabriel is dead?"

"I'm afraid so. Mason Webber shot him last night on the pier as we were trying to get away. Then he set fire to the boat we were on and forced us into the water."

The barista called the mayor's name, but she didn't seem to notice.

"I can't believe Gabriel is dead. Are you certain?"

"I watched him get shot. He fell into the lake and didn't resurface."

The barista called her name again and Holly nudged her. "Mayor, your coffee is ready."

A deep voice startled them both. "Mayor Banks? Is something wrong? Your coffee is ready."

The mayor looked up and Holly glanced at the man who had addressed her. She felt the mayor stiffen as her own legs went as limp as two wet noodles.

However, Mayor Banks rebounded quickly and pasted on a smile. "Officer McDaniels, thank you. I guess I was so caught up in my conversation that I didn't even hear my name." She slipped easily back into her witty, charming personality, took her drink and raised it to him. "Thank you so much."

Holly glanced at the man and wished she could become invisible. She recognized him and was certain he would know her, too. She turned her head, praying he wouldn't look closely at her.

The mayor was quick to intercede, diverting the officer's attention away from Holly. "I appreciate your concern, Officer McDaniels. It's so good to know the NPD is looking out for its citizens."

"Yes, ma'am. Whatever we can do to help." He turned and glanced at Holly. "Have we met before?"

"I don't think we have," she said then quickly moved to the counter to feign examining the muffins in the case.

"We're fine here," the mayor insisted. "Thanks again for asking."

He nodded then picked up his coffee and headed for the door. "Good to see you again, Mayor."

"You, too." She waved at him then glanced back at Holly. "It's not safe here. We should arrange to meet elsewhere."

Suddenly the bell on the door sounded and Holly glanced up. Officer McDaniels was back.

"Hey, I do know you!" he called, rushing toward Holly. He grabbed her arm, digging in his fingers deep.

"You're Jim Mathis's widow who was kidnapped from the med center."

She jerked her arm away from him. "I was not kidnapped. I was rescued."

He ignored her remarks and pulled out his radio. "I have a location on the kidnapping victim from yesterday. I'm at Rosie's Coffee Café."

"Roger," came the voice on the other end. Then another advised, "Sending backup," and a third added, "I'm on my way."

Holly recognized the last voice.

Mason.

She tried again to jerk her arm out of his grasp, but he dug in tighter. "You're safe now, ma'am."

Panic rushed through her. "I know you mean well and you think you're doing the right thing, but I have to leave now. I can't be here when he arrives."

"When who arrives?"

"Mason! He tried to kill me. I can't be here when he arrives."

The mayor stepped in and addressed the officer. "Maybe you should release her. I'm sure she'll calm down then."

"Excuse me, Mayor, but I'm just doing my job. This woman has been through a traumatic event."

"Yes, I have," Holly insisted, "but it wasn't because of Blake. It was Mason. He tried to kill me."

"I'm sure Officer Webber didn't try to harm you. He was only trying to help you. He told me so himself."

"He's a liar," she cried. "He's going to kill me." She didn't know if Officer McDaniels was honestly trying to help her or if he was in cahoots with Mason. It didn't matter. Either way, she had to get away from him before Mason arrived.

"Officer McDaniels, remove your hands from this young woman now," the mayor insisted, but McDaniels didn't budge.

Holly glanced around the café at the stunned faces of the patrons, who probably didn't know what to think. "Somebody help me, please!" she begged. "Please!"

She scanned every face in the room, settling on each one, hoping for a smidgeon of help. They were all shocked and concerned, but no one was going to interfere with a police officer. That was until she landed on one familiar face in the room. How had she not seen him enter and take a seat? He'd blended into the surroundings and no one had spotted him, not even her.

Now he locked eyes with her, his gaze steady and reassuring. He broke eye contact and moved toward her, coming up behind Officer McDaniels.

"She doesn't want to go with you," Blake told him.

Officer McDaniels looked irritated and turned, probably expecting to pacify some stranger with his badge and gun. Instead his eyes widened in surprise. He released her and reached for his gun, but Blake was faster and stopped his hand.

"I didn't do what you think," he said. "Mason tried to kill me, tried to kill both of us. I stopped him. He's out of control, McDaniels. You have to realize that." Officer McDaniels didn't budge and his face didn't change. "He killed Jimmy," Blake said. "He told me as much."

McDaniels's eyes flitted back and forth, weighing

Blake's words, but then he snapped at Blake. "You're a liar and corrupt."

"You're wrong. Mason is the dirty cop. Mason and Chief Waggoner and who knows who else on the force. Maybe you're part of it, too, for all I know."

McDaniels reached for his gun and Blake grabbed him. They struggled while Holly grabbed the mayor and crouched by a table for safety.

"Come to my office," the mayor whispered to her. "I can help you."

"It's not safe."

"No, it will be fine." She handed Holly her card. "Go to the parking garage under the courthouse and call this number. Tell my secretary that your name is Meredith Morgan. I'll tell her I'm expecting your call and to put you right through. I'll come down the back elevator and get you. No one will see." She glanced at Blake and Officer McDaniels struggling. "Of course, first you have to get away from here."

Blake got behind McDaniels and shoved him forward into a table, where he went sliding to the floor. Blake reached for Holly's hand. "Let's get out of here."

Holly grabbed his outstretched hand and followed him through the door. He pulled her down the sidewalk and around the building to where he had parked the pickup. She hopped into the passenger seat while he slid in behind the wheel. He quickly started the engine and they roared away.

Holly glanced through the back window and saw Officer McDaniels scanning the area, but knew even if he spotted them he wouldn't pursue. There was no way he would catch them now.

She sighed with relief that they'd escaped and felt a wave of admiration that Blake had managed to keep her safe once again. "Where did you come from? I didn't even see you enter the coffee shop."

"I'm glad I did. What did the mayor say when you approached her?"

She pulled out the card. "She wants to help us. She's on our side."

She saw his shoulders relax and he nodded. "Good. It's about time someone was."

"She said to call this number and she'll meet us in the parking garage."

"We'll head back to Dave's and lay low for a few hours. I'm sure they'll be watching her closely after this morning's incident."

She agreed and settled back into the seat. Things were finally starting to look up for them. If Mayor Banks could use her influence to get them out of town then everything would be okay. Holly almost believed it.

Almost.

He rounded the corner and Blake tensed. Holly gulped as she counted four police cars sitting in Dave's yard, their lights flashing. Blake slowed the truck then pulled over to the curb. Dave was being led out of the house in handcuffs while Chief Waggoner stood back and watched. She didn't see Mason and assumed he'd responded to the coffee shop when McDaniels had placed the call.

Blake's brow furrowed and a scowl formed on his face.

Holly felt his pain. "What can we do? How can we help him?"

"We can't, not now. The only way we help him is to get out of this town and get to the real law."

Blake jammed the pickup into Reverse and backed up to turn around. "I'm getting real tired of playing this game. Looks like our meeting with the mayor is about to get moved up a few hours."

Blake didn't like how deserted the garage was, but he supposed that was the point. However, he couldn't help but be cautious. Mayor Banks hadn't appointed Chief Waggoner—her predecessor had—yet she'd kept him on when she'd taken office. Did she not suspect the corruption of the department began at the top?

He glanced at Holly sitting nervously beside him in the truck. She'd held up amazingly through this ordeal, but her weariness was evident on her face. She pushed dark hair from her eyes, pinning it behind her ear and gave him a smile that kicked his pulse up a notch. *Get a grip,* he told himself. He was acting like a teenager with a crush. It would be so simple to fall for her, but he couldn't take a risk on love again.

He thought most women would be crying by now, ready to throw in the towel, but she'd stepped forward, insisting on going into the convenience store and then the coffee shop to approach the mayor. It had been incredibly bold of her—downright brave—especially after all she'd been through. He admired her gumption. And even when McDaniels had busted her, she hadn't cowered. She'd taken her last chance to speak to the mayor.

Too easy to fall, Lord. I need Your help to stop it.

"How are you holding up?" he asked her.

She shrugged and then sighed. "I'm hanging in there. What choice do I have?" She gave him a curious look. "Do you think this is a trap?"

He was surprised she had thought of that. Yes, he did wonder if it was a trap. He was always looking for deviousness behind every façade. But he'd never expected her to make that connection.

"She seemed too eager to help," Holly offered. She glanced at the elevator. "I just wonder who is going to come through those doors and what they'll want of us."

He pulled out his gun and checked it. "I'm ready for whatever it is."

He wished he felt as confident as he'd implied. He was ready for a gunfight, no problem, but it was the wondering, the trying to figure out who he could trust, that was getting really old. Ever since Miranda, the *not knowing* was what ate him up inside. But this was the job he had signed up for. His job was to ferret out corruption—and corrupt people didn't often advertise their dirty deeds.

They heard the hum of the elevator and Blake tensed. He felt Holly tense, as well, beside him. They got out of the pickup and moved toward the elevator. It dinged when it hit the bottom floor then the doors slid open. Blake raised his gun, ready for an ambush, but it was only Mayor Banks inside. She gasped when she saw the gun aimed at her head and Blake quickly slid it back into its holster.

"What is this?" she asked, her hand on her chest as if to steady her racing heart.

"Sorry, Mayor," he said apologetically. "We can't be too careful."

"You didn't trust me?"

"With all due respect, Mayor, we can't trust anyone right now."

Understanding dawned on her face and she nodded. "Of course. I apologize for my tone." She motioned toward the elevator. "My predecessor, Mayor Johnson, was a little too full of himself. He didn't think he should have to interact with the staff. He had this private elevator built on taxpayer funds. I would tear it out but I refuse to spend another dime of public funds to do it."

They stepped inside the elevator and she pressed the only button there. "It connects directly to my office with no other stops along the way."

The elevator whirred as it moved upward. It stopped and the doors opened. Mayor Banks stepped out into her office and Blake and Holly followed. He had his hand on his gun, still cautiously scanning the area, on alert for any signs of deception. The large room had windows lining one side, but she'd thought to close the blinds. Good. A large desk sat in the center of the room but there were also chairs and a couch making up another seating area.

"I still can't believe Gabriel is dead. After our encounter this morning, I turned on the radio. The news was reporting his death. He was a good man and an asset in ending this fight against corruption in my town." She eyed Blake. "They named you as his killer."

He wasn't surprised by that, but they didn't have time for him to rail against the injustice of it all. "I'm sorry for your loss," Blake told her, "but we need your help. Mason and Chief Waggoner are still after us."

"Yes, Mason showed up at the coffeehouse just after you two left. He was quite livid that Officer McDaniels let you get away." She sat behind her desk. "He questioned me for nearly forty-five minutes about what you wanted."

"What did you tell him?" Blake asked.

"The truth…with a twist. I told him you asked me for help, but I'd heard on the news that you had murdered Gabriel and I was too frightened. He believed me, I think. He seemed very smug that I was frightened. He and Chief Waggoner have enjoyed intimidating me these past few months."

"They're probably still watching you, though. You should be extra careful. Don't go anywhere alone and make sure you're not seen meeting with us. Do they know about the private elevator?"

"I feel certain they do."

"So they might have seen us already," Holly said.

Blake shook his head. "No, I made sure no one was around. That garage doesn't have good sight lines. Anyone who wanted to spy on us would have had to be on the bottom level. We're okay." He slid into a chair. "You said you could help us. Do you have a way out of town? A private tunnel under the lake maybe?" He laughed as he asked the last question, but considering the private elevator to her office, it wouldn't surprise him to find out that one existed.

She took his comment for what it was, a jest. "I wish there were. It won't be that easy I'm afraid. They've got patrols blocking all the roads out of town and the harbor patrol on alert. I don't have my own ship but I have some friends I can ask to borrow one. The lake is still your best chance to slip out of town unnoticed."

"What about flying out?" Holly asked.

"Our television station is too small to afford a helicopter and the hospital has to call in the one from Little Rock when they need to medevac someone out. We do have an airport, but it's small and mostly used for tourists flying in during the peak season.

"There are only a few people in town with a plane. Bill Baxter is the first to come to mind, but he can't be trusted. He's big buddies with Chief Waggoner. I can try feeling out Alex Milton to see if he might be amiable to help. He owns a string of shops on the strip and he had some problems with looters this past season. The police were not helpful in protecting his businesses. He might be someone we can count as a friend."

Blake nodded. "That's a good idea, but be careful."

"Don't worry. You're not the only one with something to lose here, Officer Michaels. But I also have quite a lot to gain. These men are ruining my town. They're opportunists—exploiting my town for everything they can get. I won't allow them to win."

He nodded. "Thank you, Mayor. We appreciate your help."

"You're welcome. Be sure to write down your phone

number so I can contact you easily when I hear back from my contacts. Now, what else can I do?"

"We need to figure out who else on the force is corrupt. I've been gathering evidence since I arrived in town and emailing it to myself. I need to access those files. I'll need a computer, a printer and a place to work."

"Of course. I'll have the conference room cleared for you and post a notice that it's occupied. No one will bother you. My staff is all loyal to me, but I would still be careful who sees you."

"Of course. We'll be discreet."

She pressed a buzzer on her phone. "Stephen, will you come in here, please?" She got up and walked to the door.

A tall, thin man with glasses entered. "Please have the conference room cleared. These two are going to be working in there and they don't want to be disturbed." She turned to Blake and Holly. "Stephen will see to your needs while I go about my business as mayor. I don't want to give any appearance that I've had any contact with you, just in case they are watching me." She must have seen the question on Blake's mind. "Don't worry. All my staff is loyal, but Stephen is my closest associate. He can be trusted."

Stephen nodded at them. "If you'll follow me, I'll show you both to the conference room."

Holly looked to him for assurance and Blake nodded. They'd made the decision to trust the mayor, so they had to do so. "You'll be sure to let me know if any of your contacts work out."

"Of course. And you'll let me know if you make any inroads into your investigation."

Blake and Holly followed Stephen to the conference room. A large table, chairs, a whiteboard and two computers were at their disposal.

Blake nodded. "This should do." He thanked Stephen, but felt he should do more than take the mayor's word that Stephen could be trusted. "Has Mayor Banks filled you in on all that is going on here?" Blake asked him.

He straightened his glasses and nodded. "She has."

Holly stepped up. "How do you feel about what she's doing helping us?"

He took a deep breath then straightened his glasses again. "Well, I'll be honest with you. I don't like it. She takes too many risks and your being here is a huge risk. She's already received death threats for her attempts to bring in outside help to clean up the town. She ignores them all and pretends they don't bother her, but I know they do. She's frightened of those men."

Holly smiled. "Yet she continues fighting for what she believes in. I believe that's the definition of bravery."

He frowned and looked at her. "Or recklessness."

"It's clear you care deeply for her and don't like the risks she's taking. So why do you continue working with her?"

"Because someone has to watch out for her and she certainly won't do it herself. I'll have some food brought in to you soon. I've told the rest of the staff that you're consultants. No one will bother you and my office is just down the hall if you need anything."

"Thank you, Stephen," Holly said.

He walked out and left them alone. Holly turned to Blake, her gaze questioning. "So what now?"

He pulled up a chair to the computer. "Now we start going over the files I've collected." Blake opened the laptop and pulled up a free email website but paused as the log-in screen popped up. His fingers hovered over the keys the way they always did. He glanced at Holly, who was watching him, waiting for him to perform the simple task of typing in a screen name. Only it wasn't so simple—especially not in front of Holly.

She glanced at him curiously with that "did you forget your login information" look and he felt his face redden.

"This is an old account," he explained. "I don't ever use it so when I needed a safe place to upload files from the police database, I thought of it."

"Okay." He could see the questioning in her face.

It was embarrassing now that she was here looking over his shoulder and watching. He typed in the words "Blake N Miranda Wedding Details" and her eyes widened before she turned her gaze away. He quickly typed in the password and pulled up the account, wishing he'd cleaned out all of the wedding nonsense, but he hadn't, just as he'd been unable to delete the account altogether.

His emails popped up. He'd been scanning and copying questionable files for months and uploading them to this email for safekeeping. He started opening them and clicking on the files, sending them to the printer for her to examine.

"I've spent my spare time since I arrived in Northshore going through police reports and looking for anomalies. These are the ones I've found. We need to go through them and look for patterns—officers who were involved, victims' names that appear over and over, possibly even locations that might stand out. If we can't get out of town, then our focus needs to be on finding out who is behind this. It might be the only thing that keeps us alive."

SIX

A few hours later Holly closed her eyes. She needed a break from the computer screen. She glanced over at Blake, who was reading through reports and making a list of names on a legal pad. He'd been embarrassed about his email username. She thought of the story he'd told her about his fiancée's betrayal and subsequent murder. She shuddered to think of the pain he'd been through.

Losing someone you loved was hard enough, but discovering she had betrayed him must have made the loss close to unbearable. It broke her heart to think Blake had suffered through that. Yet she knew from accidentally overhearing his conversation with the pastor that he'd turned to God to help him through it. It obviously hadn't done him any good. He was still suffering.

No, that's you, Holly.

She was the one still dealing with Jimmy's death. Just when she'd tried to make a restart on her life, it had knocked her down again. Sometimes, it felt like God was not only missing from her side, but that He was actively working against her.

She couldn't continue to hold on to this anger she'd been carrying around.

"Have you found something?" Blake asked, and only then did she realize she'd been staring into space.

"Just giving my eyes a break. Have you found anything?"

He stood and walked to her, taking the chair beside her so she could see the writing on the legal pad in his hand. But he was so close she could smell the clean scent of the soap he'd showered with this morning and feel the hardness of his muscles. *Focus on the data, Holly,* she chided herself. She was acting like a teenager instead of a grown woman. This man was off-limits to her. She'd already made the decision that she couldn't—she wouldn't—fall in love with another man who risked his life every day in the name of justice. She had to guard her heart.

She tried to focus instead on the writing on the pad and the words he was saying.

"I've made a list of names from your husband's journal as well as names from my own files. These are the ones that are on both lists—so these men are more than likely working with Mason."

She saw names of men she'd known for years. Her stomach drew into knots as she realized they'd gone corrupt or might have had something to do with Jimmy's death.

"So what is our next move?" she asked him.

He sighed and tossed the pad aside. "If I had more manpower or more time, I would check into each of these names, question them, maybe even find something to use against them in order to bargain for information about the drug ring." He sighed again. "But we just don't have that kind of time and I've lost my leverage. No one on this list is going to worry about my DEA connections when they believe I'll be dead before I can make it happen. They might just kill me themselves and be done with it. We need to find another avenue. There has to be something we're missing."

She agreed they had to find another way to bring down Mason and the men working with him. She read through the notes Matt had emailed to Blake about the drug Trixie: making the rounds throughout the Southeast…very dangerous…synthesized…targeted and sold to kids…the main manufacturing and distribution plant was supposedly right in Northshore. Jimmy would have been enraged when he'd found out, and a sense of sadness touched her that he hadn't felt he could share this with her. Had he felt alone in this discovery? And why hadn't he come to her with his suspicions?

She flipped a page and saw a list of ingredients the DEA had deciphered for the drug Trixie. Her eyes skimmed it, stopping on one name she recognized. Her heart dropped at the sight and for the first time she wondered if there was a greater reason that Mason had targeted her than simply being Jimmy's widow.

Blake must have noticed her tense because he put down the papers he was reading and leaned over her. "Did you find something?"

"Maybe." She pointed to the list of ingredients. "This one, hydrochloric acid, is a main ingredient in a cleanser we use at the hospital. I recently noticed an invoice that showed we'd ordered much more than we needed. I brought it to the attention of Accounts Payable, but they assured me it was a billing error that was being corrected."

"A billing error that works in the favor of whoever is manufacturing Trixie."

She nodded, realizing he understood her line of thinking. "That's a dangerous chemical, Blake. We use it to disinfect." She shuddered. "I can't believe they're actually putting that into something that they're giving to kids."

"Greed makes people do strange things. Whoever is behind this has to know the risks and just doesn't care. Who did you speak to in Accounts Payable?"

"Sherri Livingston. The odd thing is the invoice came to me in error. Someone in the mailroom made a mistake. Normally, I would never have seen it. I'm not sure anyone would have, except her."

She caught another whiff of his masculine scent and found she missed it when he straightened. She enjoyed having him close, feeling his breath on her skin. The longing for someone was familiar, but it had changed. She wasn't just longing for someone. She wanted *him*, Blake Michaels.

It was crazy. He was too much like Jimmy—stepping into danger so easily without a thought about risk to life or limb. He'd chosen a career that put his life at risk every day and he'd volunteered for this dangerous mission. She couldn't allow herself to fall for Blake. The risk to her already damaged heart wasn't worth it. Was it?

She shook off her thoughts and continued. "I've been assuming Mason targeted me because of Jimmy. Is it possible seeing this invoice and questioning Sherri is the real reason he wants me dead?"

Blake rubbed the stubble on his face and nodded. "It could be, but that would have to mean that Sherri is involved. Or it could have been what she said, a simple billing error."

Holly shook her head. "That seems unlikely when I look at this list. Someone ordered that stock."

"It's bigger than that," he said. "Whoever unloaded it would have had to ask questions, especially when the inventory they'd just unloaded disappeared from the warehouse. The question is who picked it up and moved it? And who would have noticed when they did?"

She glanced at the sheet again and felt her heart fall. Was everyone in town corrupt?

Suddenly the door burst open and Stephen ran into the room. "The police just pulled up."

Blake and Holly ran to the window and looked out. Four police cars had stopped in front of the courthouse with their lights flashing. Several men got out and she spotted Mason and Chief Waggoner among them, heading up the steps.

"They've found us again," Holly cried.

"Where's Mayor Banks?" Blake asked Stephen.

"She's heading down to talk to the chief. She wants you two to use the elevator in her office to get out of the building."

"She told me the chief knows about the elevator. Won't he have it covered?"

"I don't know, but you have to try. We cannot be found hiding you from the police."

They went back for their paperwork then Blake grabbed Holly's hand and pulled her along. She followed, double-timing it to keep up with Blake's long-legged pace. They ran through the mayor's office to the private elevator and Blake pressed the door to open it, pulling out his gun and preparing for battle as the doors opened.

Holly felt him relax a little to see that the elevator was empty, but he kept the gun out as he ushered her inside and hit the down button. She pressed herself against the back corner as Blake planted himself front and center and readied his weapon to fire the moment the doors slid open. He wasn't taking any chances. She closed her eyes as the elevator descended and found herself praying. *God, please keep us safe.*

The elevator stopped and the door slid open. Blake stepped cautiously out, his gun still at the ready. He motioned for her to follow him and she did, staying behind him as they moved through the garage.

Suddenly a light flashed and Blake spun toward it.

He saw a police cruiser, its lights flashing, driving through the garage and heading toward their level.

He pulled her to the back wall and checked several cars, hoping to find one with an open door. Breaking a window wasn't an option just yet. It would make too much noise and alert the police officer in the cruiser.

Blake spotted a storage room and hurried over, pushing a brick out from in front of the door and motioning

Holly inside. She went in and he followed, closing the door. It wasn't a long-term option since the police might start searching the garage if they suspected Blake and Holly were there, but for now it was their best recourse.

She was close enough for him to feel her pulse racing. Slowly, surely, her breathing slowed and she started to calm. He wanted to reassure her that everything was going to be fine, but the words wouldn't come.

The truth was that—again—he didn't know how they were going to get out of this. Chief Waggoner and Mason had been thorough in locking down the town. They'd blocked all their paths out and somehow continued to find them wherever they were hiding. But the desire to reassure her was just as strong as his desire to protect her. He didn't know where that was coming from but it felt warm and familiar.

Easy, he reminded himself. *You can't go down that road again.*

She was too much like Miranda, strong and independent. That was what had gotten him into trouble with Miranda. But he didn't want some wimpy woman by his side, either. He admired Holly's strength and courage. And he was glad she wasn't cowering. Not only did it make it easier to keep her safe, but it also endeared her to him in a way he hadn't expected.

Holly lifted her head and glanced up, giving him a slight smile as if she knew the truth that everything was probably not going to be fine, but she appreciated his reassurance. He liked that, too.

She understood that wallowing in doubt did no good. It wasn't over until it was over. Until the end came, they had hope. They had hope in one another, in his Ranger friends, and most importantly, hope in Jesus. He would see them both through this journey. His faith gave him the most hope. He clung to it. Needed it. Relied on it to keep him going just as he had through the ambush and afterward, through the ordeal with Miranda and through his investigation into the Northshore PD.

His phone buzzed at his hip and he pulled it out. It was a text message from Mayor Banks.

Stephen is bringing a van to pick you up while I distract the police. He will get you to a safe place.

Blake peeked out the door and spotted a white van approaching with Stephen behind the wheel. He still didn't know if he trusted him but right now wasn't the time to debate the matter. Stephen was sticking his neck out to help them, and they didn't have much in the way of options.

He pulled to a stop in front of the storage room door and slid open the side door of the van.

"Let's go," Blake whispered to Holly. "Run toward the van and jump inside. I'll be right behind you, covering you in case anyone spots us."

She nodded and when he opened the door she took off running. He followed, but even though he could see the police lights, the cruiser was still on the other side of the garage. He hopped inside the van, slid the door closed and barked for Stephen to go.

Stephen put the van into gear and drove away, heading out of the garage and onto a back street.

They were several blocks from the courthouse before Blake breathed a relieved sigh. "That was too close. Thank you, Stephen."

"How did you know where we were hiding?"

"I saw the brick was moved and guessed. I put it there because I was worried someone might hide there to try to ambush the mayor."

"I'm glad you did," Blake told him.

The mayor's associate kept his eyes on the road, but his voice was terse when he spoke again. "I didn't do it for you. I did it for Mayor Banks. She has this crazy notion of helping you two and it's going to get her arrested or possibly worse. I've tried to tell her she can't go up against Chief Waggoner."

"I imagine she can handle herself pretty well," Blake stated, trying to reassure the man.

He didn't accept the reassurance. "She takes too many risks. I'm no fool. Waggoner is dangerous and the force is corrupt. We all know it."

"She's fighting for her town, Stephen," Holly explained. "I can see you care about her very much, but she's doing the right thing standing up to injustice."

"And if she gets herself killed? Where will the town be then? Who will be left to fight for it? She's too important to put herself in danger the way she's done."

Holly touched his shoulder in a manner more reassuring than Blake could ever be. "I'm sure she'll be fine. I know it's difficult to watch the people we love take risks we might consider foolish, but I've learned it's just who they are. They can't stop fighting any more than they can stop breathing."

Blake realized she was talking about Jimmy and saw the pain on her face. She'd lost him, yet she realized that she couldn't have changed him. He knew a lot of people—mostly loved ones of his Ranger friends—hadn't understood that personality trait that pushed them to step into a firefight when others would just sit and be quiet. Miranda had certainly never understood it and his work had been a source of conflict between them.

The cell phone on the dash beeped and Stephen glanced at the screen. "It's a video message from Emily from the office."

He pressed the play button and they saw it was a video of the confrontation between Mayor Banks and Chief Waggoner on the courthouse steps. The video started in the middle of the two town leaders shouting at one another. Mayor Banks called the chief corrupt while he accused her of undermining his authority and interfering with a police investigation. It quickly escalated until she slapped Chief Waggoner and several officers dragged her kicking and screaming into a police car.

Stephen paled. "I knew something like this was going to happen." He glanced at Blake and Holly, clearly blaming them for the mayor's arrest.

It was a bad situation, Blake knew. Their only ally had been arrested and jailed, but he also knew bad things happened in a war and they were most definitely in a war situation. "She's a strong lady," Blake told him. "She can take care of herself."

"My town is erupting into chaos," he said. "I need to go check on her. Where can I drop you?"

Blake instructed him to drop them off at the next corner. Stephen pulled the van to the curb and Blake opened the door, but before he hopped out, he handed Stephen a note with their cell phone number written on it.

"In case you need to reach us," he said.

Stephen took it then waited for them to get out and close the door before turning the van around and driving away.

"I hope she'll be okay," Holly stated.

Blake nodded, knowing she probably wouldn't be, but he didn't tell her that. He didn't really have to. "Me, too."

All he knew at the moment was that Chief Waggoner had managed to cut off another avenue of help for them. They were on their own again and time was running out.

"I don't like this," Blake said as they stood outside a rear employee entrance to the hospital, where he'd parked another car—this one a small sedan—they had borrowed from an unsuspecting stranger.

Holly slipped on her hat and pushed it low to cover her face. "I'll be fine."

"I don't like the idea of you going in there alone." He placed a gentle hand on her shoulder and she felt anxiousness pour off him. He didn't like splitting up.

"I don't, either, but we need this." She stared up into his face and saw apprehension in his blue eyes. He wanted to be in there with her and she wanted that, too, but that was the reason she needed to get inside and retrieve her access card. Not only could she use it to open any outside door into the hospital, but she could also use it to get into other areas of the hospital that were off-limits to non-employees. "My card is in my locker and we need it if we want to get into Sherri's office unnoticed."

He blew out a frustrated breath. "Be careful."

"I'll be back in ten minutes," she said then turned to head around the corner to the ER entrance. She wished she could slip on her sunglasses to hide more of her face, but at this time of night they would only draw more attention to her.

God, please don't let anyone see me.

She took a deep breath and stepped through the automatic double doors that led into the ER. She recognized the people behind the admissions desk but they appeared to be busy so she lowered her head and walked through the waiting room.

The doors leading to the treatment area had automatic locks and a keypunch entry. She knew the code, but didn't want the security guard, Charlie, to see her enter it and question her. She'd worked with him before and knew he often got caught up watching the television mounted on the wall in the waiting area. She picked up a magazine and flipped through it, casting glances his way. When she spotted his gaze go to the TV, she moved toward the doors and punched in the access code. They opened and she slipped quickly through.

She kept her head low. If anyone recognized her, it would be someone here. She worked with many of these people every day. She breathed a sigh of relief when she spotted the employee break area. She reached for the handle and was pulling the door open when a voice called her name.

"Holly!"

She stopped and turned, her heartbeat ramping up and panic racing through her. Blake had been afraid this would happen. She wished he was there. He would know how to react. Should she run? Or turn and face the consequences?

"Holly, is that you?"

She turned and was relieved to see Marcy, the friend whose apartment she and Blake had used.

"Marcy, I'm so glad it's you."

Marcy threw her arms around Holly. "I can't believe you're here. The news is saying you were abducted."

Holly drew away then pulled her into the break room. "Don't you believe it, Marcy. It's not true."

"That cop friend of yours—Mason—told me all about it. He said it was a rogue cop on the force and that I should contact him if I heard from you."

Holly's grip dug into Marcy's arm as she reached for her cell phone. "Don't, Marcy. He cannot know I've been here. Mason is the one trying to kill me. He attacked me in the parking lot as I was leaving work. If Blake hadn't intervened, he would have killed me right then."

"Who's Blake?"

"He's a cop on the force, but he's been working undercover for the DEA and has discovered much of the police force here is dirty. There's a massive drug manufacturing ring operating out of Northshore. They're targeting kids, Marcy. Kids! And the police are involved.

"We've been trying to get out of town, out of their jurisdiction, but they've got all the roads blocked. They're hunting us."

"That's terrible," Marcy said. "But why would you come back here?"

"It's a long story, but I need my access card from my locker."

A frown formed on her face. "I hate to tell you this, Holly, but the police cleared out your locker. They said it was for evidence."

They went to her locker and Holly noticed that the combination lock was gone, probably cut off. She opened the door and saw that Marcy was right. The locker was empty.

Disappointment filled her. They needed that card, but it was gone and so was their only chance of getting into Sherri's office and looking for evidence.

"Use mine," Marcy said, slipping it into Holly's hand.

Holly clutched it, thankful to her friend, then gave her a big hug. "You don't know what this means to me."

Marcy eyed her. "This Blake fellow...do you trust him?"

She didn't even have to consider the question. Her answer came immediately without hesitation. "Absolutely, I trust him." She knew it was true. She'd grown to trust Blake completely and she had no doubt that he was her only chance for getting out of this town alive.

That was all Marcy needed to hear. "Stay safe, Holly." She adjusted the hat on Holly's head then headed out. "I'll make sure the coast is clear so you can slip by unnoticed." She disappeared through the doors and Holly saw her stop a nurse heading for the break room. Holly was able to slip by them without being seen and headed quickly toward the back hallway to the access door where Blake was waiting. She slipped the card through the reader and the door unlocked.

Blake hurried inside, agitation pouring off him. "I was getting worried. What took you so long?"

"I'll explain later." She held up the card. "I got it. Let's go."

Coming here had been a risk, but it was one they'd had to take. They needed to see the billing invoices, and Holly grew more and more excited as they neared the hallway that housed Sherri Livingston's office. She used the access card to open the hallway doors that were always locked and again on the suite of offices that housed the billing department.

"It's down here on the right," Holly told him, turning to look to make certain no one had seen them.

Blake stopped in front of the door marked Sherri Livingston, Accounts Payable Supervisor. There was no place to swipe the card, but the door was locked so he pulled out a knife and quickly jimmied the lock and the door slipped open. Holly realized she'd been holding her breath as the door opened, but released it when no alarm sounded.

He ushered her inside and closed the door behind them.

Holly hurried to Sherri's desk and started digging through her inbox. Finding nothing, she moved to the file drawers on either side of the desk while Blake pulled open the big filing cabinet and began search-ing. The drawers revealed nothing helpful, so Holly turned on Sherri's computer.

All the hospital staff's logon information started with their extension number and Holly was quickly able to figure it out. However, when it asked for a password, she stopped. She had no idea what Sherri's password was and no idea how to find it. She searched through the drawers again and around the computer, hoping Sherri had written it down somewhere the way some people did. She didn't find it. But the handmade, framed photo on her desk gave Holly an idea. It was a picture of her daughter with her name written in dried pasta on the frame. Many people used their kids' names as pass-words so Holly took a chance and typed it in.

The screen popped up.

Blake leaned over her. "Pull up her saved docu-ments."

Holly did as he instructed, checking for document titles featuring the name of the company that fur-nished their cleaning supplies. She finally found one and double-clicked on it to open it up. Just as she'd sus-pected, the billing error appeared on this invoice, as well, and Sherri had made a notation on the scanned copy that it had been paid in full with hospital funds. She pulled up another invoice from the same company for a different month and saw that the same amount had been ordered and paid for. She quickly printed out several copies to prove Sherri had been actively hiding the large order of supplies and fraudulently using the hospital's money to cover the expense.

"What should we do now?" Holly asked him.

"What's the fastest way to the loading dock? I'd like to get a look at their records, as well."

She nodded and started to point out the direction for him, but footfalls outside the door caught her attention. "Someone's coming," she whispered.

She shut down the computer while he clicked off the lights. Blake peeked out the door then whispered, "Security," to her. Holly's heart thudded in her chest. It would be disastrous if they were discovered in there, but she had to wonder why they'd come. Was this a routine check of the offices, or had they somehow been alerted when she'd used Marcy's access card to enter the suite?

The footsteps on the tiled floor outside grew louder. Blake softly closed the door again then pulled her across the room and to the floor, crawling under the desk. Holly squeezed in beside him. Her breath caught when the door opened and a beam of light swept the room. She could see it and crouched closer against the desk. Her head was lying on his chest and she could hear the steady beat of his heart. No panic for him. He stayed calm and cool under pressure, and she liked that. He wrapped his arm around her waist and pulled her tightly against him as the beam of light continued to sweep.

Holly held her breath again and felt panic begin to rise inside her. If they were caught here, they might be handed over to the police. Mason would surely enact his wrath on them then. Blake must have sensed her rising agitation because he tightened his grip and locked eyes with her, his eyes somehow conveying a reassurance that everything would be okay. She was already calming down as the security guard closed and locked the door, leaving them once again in darkness.

"Are you all right?" Blake whispered, his warm breath gentle on her ear.

"I'm okay."

She crawled out from beneath the desk and he did the same, stopping for only a moment to survey her, decide obviously that she was indeed okay, and then move to the door. He softly opened it and peeked into the hallway.

"It's clear. We need to go now before he comes back this way."

Holly hurried down the hall toward the loading docks. She knew they'd once again escaped detection, and it was all because of Blake.

Thank You, God, that he's on my side.

But now she wondered about the access card in her pocket. Had her best friend ratted her out to security?

She couldn't believe that and decided it must have just been a coincidence that he'd come by. After all, he hadn't searched the office, only scanned it with his light.

While she was still wondering about Marcy, they arrived at the loading dock. It appeared to be empty. The crew had probably gone home for the day. They approached the office and it, too, was empty. Holly used the access card to unlock the door and pushed it open. She held her breath, waiting to see if an alarm would sound. None did.

He hurried inside and picked up the manifest.

"There's no record here of a shipment that large. Someone on the loading dock is working with them or being paid off to look the other way."

"We need to speak to Ben Casey. He's the loading dock manager. If a shipment came through here, he knew about it. He recently lost his wife of forty-three years to cancer. It was a long, hard struggle for him."

Blake nodded. "Losing someone you love can do strange things to a person. It's possible he's simply been too preoccupied with her illness and his own grief that someone was able to pull this off without his knowledge."

She hoped that was what it was, but even during his wife's prolonged illness, Holly knew he'd had his eye on everything. He'd told her once that the job was what kept him going; having something to focus on besides the illness had been his lifeline.

"He's a very sweet man. I hope he's not involved."

She saw the doubt in Blake's face and it didn't surprise her. It was obvious that Mr. Casey had, at the very least, known something fishy was happening on his docks. But had he been complicit or even involved in moving the chemicals? And if he was, did he have any idea they were using it to make drugs that were targeted to kids?

She sighed, realizing that at this point, very little would surprise her.

They left the loading dock with Ben Casey's address in their possession. They'd been fortunate and found a note posted on the bulletin board with his name and address. Blake supposed he'd put it there in case any of his employees needed to reach him, but he was glad he'd posted it. Blake was determined to speak with the man and find out what he knew. He knew Holly was hesitant. She wanted to believe the best in people, but he was more likely to believe the worst. He hated that about himself. It was a fallout from his experience with the ambush and, again, his betrayal by Miranda. In fact, he'd gotten to the point where his first instinct was always to expect the worst in people.

But as he slid into the driver's seat of the small sedan, he realized he wanted to believe the best in Holly. His feelings for her were changing. It was becoming a natural instinct to trust her. He was already depending on her in a way he hadn't depended on anybody since his time in the military—which made sense since they were in a fight for their lives. *Lord, guard my heart. Don't let me fall for someone unworthy of Your plan.*

He placed the key in the ignition and turned the engine. It roared to life, much louder than it should have been. It took a moment to realize it was more than just the engine he was hearing. Something flashed in the corner of his eye and he spun his head to see a huge dump truck barreling toward them. Holly saw it, too, and they reacted at nearly the same moment as the monster slammed into them.

SEVEN

Holly screamed and tried to grab for something to hold on to. She felt the metal around her start to give. The dump truck hit them on the front just near his door—an inch more his way and Blake would be dead. He pressed down on the accelerator, but the engine died. The crunching continued as they were pushed into another car, ultimately sealing off both doors for their escape.

"We have to get out," he said, reaching for his seat belt. Holly unbuckled and crawled over the seat, stopping when she realized Blake wasn't moving.

"I'm stuck," he told her, pressing the button on his seat belt with no effect. "You go! Kick out the back window and get out!"

Her eyes widened as the dump truck rammed them again. This time, without her seat belt, she went flying across the seat and slammed against the passenger window. Her head hit the glass with a thud and pain riddled through her. Nausea grabbed her and she thought she might lose consciousness. She fought it. If she passed out, she was dead, and so was Blake. But she couldn't stop the groan that escaped her lips as she moved back toward him.

"Holly! Are you okay?" She heard the terror in his voice and tried to reassure him with a gentle nod that sent waves of pain rushing through her again.

She leaned over the seat and fiddled with his seat belt, trying to get it to give.

"It's locked," Blake stated. "Just go."

"No, I'm not leaving you. Can you wriggle free of it?"

"No, it locked on impact." Fear glowed in his eyes. "Holly, you have to get out."

She wasn't going to just leave him. Outside, the truck's engine roared again as it backed up, ready to ram them once more.

"Do you have a knife on you?"

"No, I lost it in the water."

She glanced around the car for something she could use to cut the belt. Shattered pieces of glass lay on the floor and seat. She picked up one of them and used it to slice through the fabric. The sharp edges cut into her hands and stung, but she kept on going. She couldn't—she wouldn't—leave him. Relief flooded her when Blake pulled against the belt and it gave. But they weren't out of the woods yet. They still had to get out of the car. Blake wiggled around and put all his strength into kicking out the passenger window. She felt a rush of relief when it shattered.

"Go!" he said, motioning for her to go through first.

She scrambled over the seat and through the window, sliding onto the crushed car beside them then to the pavement. Blake slid through the window, too, but she saw him wince and realized he'd sliced his leg on a piece of glass. She grabbed his arm and tried to help him through as the big truck roared toward them. If they weren't out of the way when it hit, they would be crushed.

Blake shoved her to the side and jumped. Holly hit the pavement, screaming as the truck rammed again and the cars barely missed Blake's leg before slamming into the concrete wall of the building. The sound of metal crushing was deafening, and Holly knew he'd managed to get out with only seconds to spare.

Blake crawled to his feet. Blood was dripping down his face, but he grabbed her arms and pulled her up. She shuddered, realizing they would surely be dead if they'd been inside the car. But that wasn't all. Her head was still ringing from the hit she'd sustained and she wasn't all that steady on her feet.

"I need a minute," she said, trying to regain her balance.

"I'm not sure we have a minute. We have to go now." His voice held urgency and she knew he was right but worried he wouldn't be able to run with that leg. She didn't know if she could run, either, with her head spinning and nausea twisting her stomach. But she wouldn't give in to it. Somehow she was on her feet. She hurried across the parking lot, Blake limping by her side. She draped his arm over her shoulder to help carry some of his weight and he didn't protest, but Holly knew they were leaving a trail of blood behind them…a trail that would lead whoever was driving that truck right to them.

She heard the big truck's gears crack and knew the driver was following them. He roared across the parking lot, ignoring curbs and driving on the sidewalk as he aimed the truck their way. Holly noticed people emerging from the hospital, curious about the commotion. Hopefully, a crowd would frighten him away before he reached them. Even Mason—and she was certain it was Mason behind the wheel—couldn't cover up murder with an audience. But instead she noticed the few who'd ventured out running back inside, too frightened to remain.

Blake leaned on her and they rounded a corner as the dump truck rammed into a side building. She heard screams and the crack of concrete and metal, but didn't stop running. She glanced back to see the truck's door open and Mason tumble out. She heard the sound of police sirens approaching and stopped running only long enough to see Mason abandon the truck and take off into the woods.

"We can't be here when the police arrive." Blake groaned, his face contorting in pain. He motioned at a minivan in the parking lot and they hurried to it. He grabbed a rock and slammed it against the window, causing it to shatter. They slid inside and he fiddled with the ignition wires until the engine roared to life.

"Can you even drive?" she asked, uncertain by the pale color of his skin.

Again, Holly didn't like the idea of taking someone else's vehicle, but she figured it was better than getting caught and killed once the police arrived. She had no doubt she and Blake both would have an "accident" if they found themselves locked in a jail cell.

Blake slid the minivan into gear and took off out of the parking lot. Holly glanced back and saw police cars approaching the hospital from the other side of the lot. They would be busy securing the scene and taking witness statements. She felt herself start to relax as the whole incident seemed to be ending, but she knew it wasn't over. Mason had come close to killing them, closer than she could believe. She didn't know where he'd come from, or where he'd gotten the dump truck, or how he'd even known they were there.

"The construction," Blake said as if reading her mind. "He must have seen us, spotted the dump truck at the construction site and just went from there."

Blood dripped onto the seat. He was bleeding not only from the leg but from the wound in his side. "It must have reopened sliding out of the car. We need to get somewhere so I can tend to your wounds."

"I'm fine," he said, but the pale color of his face told her differently.

"Pull over," she told him. "I'll drive."

Instead of the argument she'd expected, he pulled to the curb and slid across the seat. She slipped into the driver's seat.

As she drove, her mind spun with what to do and where to go. Blake was on the seat beside her, barely holding on to consciousness. The fact that he'd voluntarily handed over the driving told her he was in bad shape. What would she do if something happened to him? She didn't even know where Mason had come from when he'd barreled into them.

It was up to her now to be strong and take care of him and that meant first of all finding a place to hide and figure out just how badly Blake was hurt. He slumped over the seat and a ripple of fear raced through her. What would she do if he was seriously hurt? Taking him back to the hospital would be as good as signing his death warrant, especially since they'd just escaped from there and the place would by now be swarming with police. But what choice would she have if he needed medical care greater than she could give him?

She racked her brain, trying to think of somewhere they could go that Mason wouldn't look for them. That ruled out her house. He would surely have it under surveillance now that he knew she'd returned there once. And she wouldn't go back to Marcy's and put her friend in any more danger.

Lord, we need a safe place. Please help me find one.

She groaned when an answer didn't come right away. That's what she got for turning to God for help. Just more proof that He was not on her side.

She pulled the minivan to the side of the road and leaned into the steering wheel. Hot tears threatened her eyes, but she pushed them away. She couldn't fall apart right now. Blake needed her to be the strong one.

She didn't have a light, but she checked his pupils and they seemed normal, yet he had lost consciousness. She didn't think he had any serious head trauma, yet when she felt his head, she found a knot forming. Blood came back on her hand when she pulled it away.

He must have hit his head on the asphalt when he leaped from the car. Add that to the fact that he was bleeding from at least two significant wounds. She needed to find a place to check out his wounds more thoroughly and they both needed rest and time to recover from this last attack.

She jumped, startled when the phone in Blake's pocket rang. She pulled it out, her hands shaking as she glanced at the screen. Only a number showed, no name, but the only person she knew who had this number was Matt. She could use someone on their side to tell her what to do.

She pushed the answer button. "Hello, Matt?"

"No, Holly, it's Chief Waggoner."

She gasped in shock. "How did you get this number?"

"The mayor's assistant, Stephen, had this number in his phone when we searched through his things."

"You arrested Stephen?" Anger bit through her. She knew the young man had done nothing to warrant an arrest…except perhaps helping Holly and Blake escape. "For what crime?"

"He and Mayor Banks are being detained for questioning."

Hot tears burned her eyes as the chief reaffirmed to her just how corrupt the NPD really was. "That doesn't give you the right to go through his phone."

"I didn't call to talk about them. It's you I'm concerned about, Holly." His voice softened, but the urgency remained in his tone. "You're in danger. You were right about Mason. He's out of control. I should have listened to you, protected you. I still can. You're one of us. You just have to come in. I'll make sure you're not harmed. That's my promise."

She glanced down at Blake. He did need medical

help and the chief's offer was tempting. Or maybe she was just so weary and so frightened that she wanted to trust Chief Waggoner. But she didn't. And she realized he hadn't said anything about protecting Blake, too.

Then she remembered what Blake had told her about Mason claiming he had friends in high places on the force. She already knew the chief was corrupt, but was he the one calling the shots? "How do I know you can control Mason? You haven't so far." Because he hadn't wanted to?

His tone took on an angry bite, confirming her suspicions. He didn't like having his authority questioned. "Don't worry about him. He'll do what I say."

So the chief was calling the shots. "What about Blake?"

"He'll be fine. Nothing has happened yet that can't be undone."

He was trying to manipulate her by using their history together as leverage, but his once-friendly voice now sounded as empty and false as his intentions truly were.

"No," she told him, then hung up before he could make any more demands. She didn't have time for his hollow promises or threats.

The phone rang again and the same number popped up, so she turned it off. Her head was pounding and she was still rattled from being thrown around in the car, but she had no time to be weak. She had to think and make decisions. Their lives depended on it. First thing on the list was medical supplies. She needed bandages to stop the bleeding. She opened the door and searched through the vehicle, hoping to find a first-aid kit. She didn't find one, which meant she would have to purchase some supplies. But did she dare risk stopping at a store with Mason and the chief after her?

She sighed. She didn't have much choice.

She slid back behind the wheel and drove until she came across a convenience store on the outskirts of town by the campgrounds. The parking lot wasn't full and it wasn't large so she thought she should be able to get in and out quickly. She checked Blake's pockets and found his wallet. Thankfully, he had cash on him because she'd long ago lost her purse and any money she'd had. She removed a few bills, eyeing the ring again. Now that she knew its story, she wanted to throw it out the window. Why did he still carry around a reminder of such pain and betrayal?

Blake was still out beside her. She bent and kissed his cheek, whispering in his ear, "I'll be right back."

She hurried inside and found the first-aid stuff she needed, then grabbed a few bottles of water and two wrapped sandwiches, realizing they hadn't eaten anything for quite a while. She approached the register.

"Nice night," the clerk commented as he rang up her items.

"Yes, it is," she agreed, hoping he wouldn't linger over the transaction. She needed to get in and out of here as quickly as possible.

"The view of the lake is amazing at night this time of year, especially from the east side of the campgrounds. Which side are you staying on?"

She stared at him, the kernel of an idea settling into her. The campgrounds would be a perfect place for them to hide out. The cabins would be nearly abandoned at this time of year. She could find one that was unoccupied and they could take shelter there for a while, at least until Blake was back on his feet. Mason might search there eventually, but for now, it was a plan.

"The east side," she told him, a smile forming on her face. *And thank you for the idea.*

She hurried back to the minivan and climbed inside, excitement bursting through her. She had a plan and that was much better than the anxious uncertainty she'd felt only minutes ago.

She headed for the campgrounds and turned in, driving deep into the woods. If Mason searched here, he would start at the front so she didn't even bother stopping at those cabins. She finally pulled up to a cabin that appeared to be unoccupied. No cars sat in front and she saw no signs of human activity—no boats, floats or grills evident.

She slid out and hurried up the steps, peering in through the window. As she expected, it was empty. She jiggled the door handle. It was locked. She ran her hands over the door frame, hoping to find a spare key, then searched the porch, checking under planters and any nook or cranny she could find. Finally she found what she was looking for hidden inside a planter. She quickly unlocked the door and pushed it open, finding a few pieces of furniture and a small kitchen. It would do.

She ran back to the minivan and drove around to the back of the cabin. She roused Blake, who was waking up. He was still groggy, but woke enough to walk to the cabin propped against her shoulder.

"Where are we?" he asked groggily.

"A cabin at the campgrounds. It's a safe place to rest."

He nodded and allowed her to lead him inside. She walked him to the couch and he slid onto it. She went back out to the van to retrieve the first-aid supplies.

"Let me check out your head," she said and he complied, leaning forward so she could examine the back of his head.

"You took quite a blow back here. How are you feeling?"

"I'm fine," he said, then tried to get to his feet. His knees buckled and he fell back onto the couch. "I'm fine," he again assured her.

"You're not fine, but you will be. I don't believe you have any permanent head trauma, but you had your clock cleaned real good. Your head will probably be buzzing for a while." She taped a bandage onto the back of his head.

She checked out his injuries and found his ankle was unbroken but was swelling from a terrible twist. His side wound had started bleeding again, and he had tiny pieces of shrapnel lodged in his back.

She lifted his shirt so she could remove them and clean the wounds, and Holly saw other, healed scars on his back. She gently touched them, wondering about each wound and how he'd suffered with them. He would have a few more now in his struggle to protect her. Somehow, she knew instinctively that he'd been protecting someone when each wound had been inflicted.

He shuddered when she touched them and she quickly pulled her hand away. "I'm sorry. I shouldn't have done that."

"It's okay," he rasped. "It's just that your hands are cold."

She turned away and began cleaning up the bandages while he pulled his shirt back down, but the images of those scars wouldn't leave her.

"How did you get those?" she asked him.

He shrugged and at first she thought he was going to brush off her question, but instead he looked at her and his face grew grim. "Remember I told you my Ranger squad was ambushed, and most of my team was killed? Well, I took six shots in the back."

Despite the fact that she'd seen the scars, hearing him say it made her shudder. "You're fortunate to be alive."

He gave her a quick "I know" nod of his head then tried again to stand, using the arms of the couch to push himself to his feet. This time, his legs cooperated and he managed to walk, favoring his injured ankle, a little unsteadily, grunting across the room before falling again into a chair a few feet away.

"I've got to get back on my feet."

"You need to rest and recover," Holly told him. "You're not a machine. Your body needs time to heal."

"I don't have time," he grunted then pushed himself to his feet again. "Mason could find us any minute."

Her hands shook and all the emotions she'd been pushing back came flooding through her. She covered her face and, unable to stop them, let the tears flow freely.

She felt Blake sit beside her on the couch and leaned into him when he wrapped his arms around her and pulled her to him. All she could think of was what she would have done if something had happened to him, if she'd been left alone again and had to face Mason by herself.

God, thank You for keeping him safe. The plea went up without her say-so, but it was true. She was so thankful that Mason hadn't killed him and, she realized suddenly, so worried that he had.

When her tears were spent, she wiped her face and pushed away from him. She glanced at him but didn't see pity or annoyance in his face even though she felt those things. She didn't want to be one of those crying, hysterical females. She was stronger than that, but here she was crying on his shoulder.

"I'm sorry," she whispered, her voice dry and hoarse. "I suppose it's all catching up with me."

He reached out and touched her face, pushing that stray strand of hair back. "You don't have to apologize, Holly. I understand what you're feeling. I went through something similar during my time as a Ranger. It's hard to stop and feel your emotions when you're fighting for your life. The emotion comes later, after everything has settled down. It's like the second wave of an attack."

She nodded. "I guess that's right."

"It's a normal reaction. Adrenaline keeps you moving and responding. It's only later that the reality of the situation hits your mind and your heart. That's the point where you start second-guessing everything."

She sniffed back more tears. "Really? Rangers second-guess themselves?"

"Sure we do. We're only human. Usually it's not about tactics. We do so much training that during a firefight the physical parts are almost instinctive. I don't have to ask myself do I fight my way out or just start shooting. I just know. It's the people that really get into your head, though. The people you help, the people you lose, even those you see while you're patrolling. Being a cop wasn't much different. Smaller weapons and fewer orders to kill." He gave her a smile to let her know he was only joking. "Seriously, people can only take so much stress, then they snap."

"How did you handle it when you were a Ranger?"

"I had Someone who could handle it for me. Jesus Christ."

She turned away. She didn't want that to be the answer. She wasn't ready to give everything to Jesus. He'd let her down too many times.

"I take it you're not a believer?"

"I grew up in church. I even walked the aisle and accepted Jesus when I was a teenager. Jimmy and I were active in the church."

"Yet I sense you're not so close to God now, are you?"

"No." She tried to bite back the anger that pulsed through her at the memory, but was sure it showed up in her tone. "Jimmy is gone. I'm sure there is a rhyme or reason for taking my husband from me, but I guess I'm not ready to hear it yet. He's gone and when I think about praying, I just get angry. I didn't think I still had any of that anger left inside me, yet it keeps manufacturing itself—reappearing just when I think I'm getting better."

She half expected him to shun her for admitting she was angry at God, but instead he nodded and pulled her close to him, his big arms wrapping her in his embrace.

"I get that," he told her. "I went through something similar when Miranda died. I wanted answers and I was so angry that she died before she could give them to me."

She closed her eyes, angry at herself for forgetting she wasn't the only one who'd suffered a loss. He'd lost his fiancée and his Ranger squad. He'd suffered so much more loss than she had, yet he was handling it so much better. Because he'd found comfort in God instead of blaming Him? That must be the reason, but she still couldn't bring herself to let go of her anger.

"When I came to Northshore, I met Pastor Dave. I wasn't really on speaking terms with God after all that had happened but, like I told you, I got involved in church to meet people and be accepted into the community. But along with reading my Bible again, I started meeting with Dave once a week for counseling, and soon realized I wasn't angry anymore. It had been like a cancer growing inside me, and God just cut it out and tossed it away."

She pushed up and looked at him, thinking again of the ring in his wallet. "Then why do you still carry the ring around with you?"

His face flushed and he seemed hesitant. "I don't know. I guess I just haven't been able to let it completely go." He stared into her face and suddenly his look changed. A dizzying current crackled between them and Holly felt her pulse begin to race. "Until now," he whispered, cupping her chin in his hands and gently kissing her.

Holly melted under the weight of him, surprised by

her intense feelings for this man. She'd come to rely on him and now she realized it wasn't just because he'd rescued her. She was falling in love with him, with his protective nature and his caring manner. Even his scars gave him a depth she found attractive. Even after all he'd suffered, he kept fighting.

She caught her breath and pushed away from him. She knew it was already too late. She'd fallen hard for this former soldier and could imagine spending her life wrapped in his arms. But the fear she'd felt at the idea of losing him hit her hard. She'd already lost Jimmy, and Blake was cut from the same cloth. He was quick to jump in to protect those who needed it, which meant he put his life in danger on a daily basis. And while she was thankful he'd taken that step with her, she just didn't know if she could build a life with someone who took those kinds of risks.

"I'm sorry, I can't," she rasped. She stared up into his face and fought the desire to melt into his arms again. "I can't deny I have feelings for you, Blake, but I've already lost someone..." She shook her head and pushed back tears that threatened. "I just can't go through something like that again. I never worried about Jimmy, but one day he didn't come home and I know I'll spend my life wondering each day if you're coming home, too."

He nodded and pulled away, running a hand through his hair and sighing. "I understand that," he told her, his voice choked with emotion. "Taking risks is part of my job. Not everyone can handle that kind of life."

"I think it's more than just part of your job. It's a lifestyle for you. It's like you said earlier. You just react. You don't think or anything. You just spring into action. I mean, you volunteered to come here to North-shore, to go undercover and step into danger when you had nothing drawing you here except a new challenge. I just—I can't do that again."

He pulled away from her and stood, his ankle still shaky and frustration rolling off him in waves. He moved to the kitchen and rubbed a hand over his jaw. "No, you're right. We need to focus on finding this drug ring and getting out of town. So…" He folded his arms and suddenly became all business. "Ben Casey. We need to question him."

He looked at her and she nodded. "Mr. Casey. There's no way he wouldn't know what was happening on his dock."

Blake nodded. "Then we need to go have a conversation with Mr. Casey."

"Yes, we do. But not tonight." She stood to face him and slipped into nurse mode. "You need to rest and get your strength back."

"I'm fine, Holly."

"No, you're not. You're weak, your head is probably still spinning and that ankle is swollen. You need to be at your best before we start confronting anyone asso-ciated with the drug ring. And what if Mason attacks again? We both need you to be ready and strong."

"Yes, nurse," he retorted giving her a slow smile to show he knew she meant well.

She went to grab the cold pack that was part of the

first-aid kit, hoping that the next time Mason confronted them, they would both be ready.

A night of rest had done wonders for him. He'd spent some time with a cold pack on his ankle and the swelling this morning was minimal. His head was clearer, too, and not just from the bump he'd sustained. Holly had been right when she'd rebuked him last night. He couldn't deny he was falling for her, but he couldn't let himself go down that road, either. She had her reasons and so did he, but the bottom line was that he didn't trust his own feelings. They'd deceived him before with Miranda. How could he trust they wouldn't let him down again?

He pulled up and parked along the curb in front of Ben Casey's house. It was early morning and a fog was lifting. He'd wanted to catch the man before he went to work, because he didn't want to have to go back to that loading dock if he could help it.

He knew Holly was hoping this man she admired wasn't involved in drug manufacturing, but he'd learned you couldn't always trust people to be who they claimed to be.

Casey seemed surprised to see Holly, and Blake wondered if he was aware yet that she was labeled a kidnapping victim. But he knew it had been on the news and the hospital staff would have been alerted about a possible kidnapping on the campus.

But his surprise seemed to stem from her approaching him outside of work as opposed to the fact that she was on the run for her life.

"What are you doing here?" he asked Holly then glanced at Blake.

Blake ignored his question and got right to the business at hand. "Mr. Casey, we need to speak with you about some abnormal activity on the loading dock."

A frown line creased his face. "What do you mean by abnormal activity?"

Holly answered him. "I came across an invoice by accident that showed a large shipment of cleaning solvent. Have you noticed any big shipments like that?"

He seemed to consider the question for a moment then shook his head. "No, nothing out of the ordinary. Just normal stuff."

"This would have been a large shipment that possibly went missing from storage," Holly pressed.

"I know every piece of freight and supplies that come through that loading dock and I don't recall anything like that. It was probably just a billing error. They charged us for inventory we didn't receive. It happens all the time. Someone hits a seven instead of a one and suddenly we're being charged for seven hundred rolls of toilet paper. It doesn't mean we received that many." He shrugged off her concerns, but Holly seemed skeptical.

She bit on her lower lip then asked him uncertainly, "Are you sure, Mr. Casey?"

He glanced from her to Blake and then back to her. "What's this about, Holly? You come to my house and question me about missing inventory and irregularities on my dock. You're a nurse and you have nothing to do with inventory. Are you trying to accuse me of something? Because I've worked at that hospital for thirty years. No one has ever questioned my integrity before."

"I don't mean to upset you," Holly said. "It's just that this is very important. We believe someone is using the hospital to funnel supplies to a drug manufacturing plant. This solvent contains a chemical used to manufacture a new synthetic drug that is being marketed to kids. Several have died after ingesting it."

His brow furrowed again. "They can do that? Use cleaning solvent to make drugs?"

Blake interceded. "They can. Drug rings have chemists that can remove the chemicals involved and reuse them for drug manufacturing."

Holly nodded as Mr. Casey looked at her, incredulous. "It's true. And someone in this town is using our hospital to do it."

Blake noticed the man's hands shaking before he slipped them into his pockets. He knew something. Blake was sure of it. But Casey gave a weary sigh and didn't give in. "I sure am sorry about what's happening, but it's not coming through my loading dock. I would know if there was any funny business going on."

"But the invoice," Holly insisted.

"Was just a billing error," Ben Casey insisted. "Now, if you'll excuse me, I need to get to work before I'm late for my shift."

He got into his car, buckled his seat belt then backed out of the driveway and disappeared down the road.

Holly turned to Blake. "He's lying. He knows something."

Blake nodded. "I got that sense, too."

"He's not a mastermind criminal. He's a nice man who has spent his career at the hospital."

"He seemed genuinely shook up when you told him what the chemicals were being used for. I doubt he knew what they were doing. They probably plied him with enough cash that he told himself he didn't have to know. I'll have Matt check into his financials and find out if any of his wife's medical bills have suddenly been taken care of or if there are any other discrepancies in his finances. I feel like if we press him with something solid, he'll crack."

She nodded. "I think you're right."

They walked back to their vehicle and she slid into the passenger's seat and buckled her seat belt. Blake knew she hoped he was correct that Mr. Casey had gotten caught up in something he had no idea about. That was the version she wanted to believe—mostly because she would have a difficult time believing anyone would purposefully poison kids. Yet he knew there were people who not only were aware of the danger they were creating, they reveled in it, and they would kill to continue doing it.

Once they were back at the campground, Blake grabbed the phone and walked out to the lake. The phone was turned off, which surprised him. He pressed the button and powered it back up.

He dialed Matt, and his friend answered right away.

"Please tell me you have some good news," Blake said.

Matt sighed. "We're being blocked at every turn. The local police are crying federal encroachment and harassment all over the news. My bosses are treading very carefully over this matter. How are you holding up?"

"Not bad. We had a run-in with Mason last night and got a little shaken up, but we're fine."

He could imagine the frown on Matt's face. "Define 'shaken up.'"

"I'm fine. Turned my ankle and hit my head, but Holly's a good nurse. She patched me up."

"Glad to hear it. Have you been able to uncover anything that might help us?"

"Holly discovered the hospital has been ordering large amounts of cleanser containing hydrochloric acid."

"That's one of the chemicals used in manufacturing Trixie."

"That's right. We believe they're shipping it to the hospital, someone in Accounts Payable is covering it up and then someone else is making sure it's moved without anyone noticing."

"Any idea who these people are?"

"Yes, the loading dock supervisor is named Ben Casey. He's worked there for thirty years, but recently lost his wife to cancer. He seemed bothered when Holly told him what the shipments were being used for. I think he's only in it for the money. Can you check out his financials? My guess is that his wife's medical bills have suddenly been taken care of."

"I'll check it out myself."

"The other is Sherri Livingston, a woman in Accounts Payable. We found some invoices showing she's paying the bills and covering the paperwork for the shipments. I'll email you pictures of those."

"Great. Have you found out where the manufacturing plant is located?"

"Not yet. Northshore isn't that big of a town, and believe me I've searched it all…or at least I thought I had. But there must be somewhere I've missed."

"I'll be honest with you, Blake. Without the location and confirmation of the plant, I'm not sure my bosses are going to approve breaching the town. They're trying to negotiate, but in private, they're talking about cutting their losses."

"They can't do that," Blake said.

"I'm afraid they can."

Blake raked a hand over his jaw. Having the DEA pull out would be devastating not only for him and Holly, but also for all the kids that these drugs would be marketed to. This was no longer only about remaining safe but about bringing down those whose nefarious plans would harm others.

God, please lead us to the answers to stop these people.

"But we're so close. If I can press Sherri and Mr. Casey, I know I can get a lead on where the plant is located. One of them must know something."

"I'll check into both of their financials. Meanwhile, you press on these people hard, Blake. I honestly don't know how much time you have left before the DEA pulls out. We need something concrete I can take to my bosses." Matt wished him well then hung up.

Blake turned back to the cabin. He knew Holly was inside waiting for him. He felt the weight of the burden they were facing pressing down on them. She was depending on him and he had to do a better job. Yet he knew he couldn't move forward with her until he stopped holding on to the past.

He pulled his wallet from his pocket and took out the ring. He'd held on to it for too long. He turned toward the water, pulled back his arm and tossed the ring in. He knew Holly was skeptical about starting a relationship with him, but he hoped she might change her mind and give them a chance. If she did, he wanted to be ready.

But first they had to get out of Northshore alive. Matt had just given him a deadline and they needed to find answers soon.

They were running out of time.

Holly unbuckled her seat belt as Blake stopped the truck at the curb in front of Ben Casey's house. It was late in the evening and the lights were on inside. His car was sitting in the driveway.

"I guess he's home," Holly said.

"I guess he is. And now that he's had some time to mull over our previous conversation, I'm going to get some answers out of him."

Blake got out and led the way to the house. He opened the screen door and knocked, but the door moved and he realized it wasn't closed all the way. He glanced at Holly and saw her surprise.

From inside, he could hear the sounds of the television and see the lights flickering.

He reached for his gun and felt Holly tense. He hoped he was overreacting and the man had just forgotten to latch the door, although he doubted anyone would be so careless in this neighborhood. He pushed open the door and glanced around, making sure to keep Holly behind him, but it only took him a moment to realize Ben Casey wouldn't be responding.

"Mr. Casey?" Holly called then moved toward the kitchen. She turned as she passed the recliner in front of the television. Her eyes widened and she rushed to the figure on the floor.

Blake knelt beside him and felt for a pulse. There wasn't one. And the gun on the ground beside him told him all he needed to know. Ben Casey was dead.

Holly hadn't yet realized it. She began CPR, but Blake knew it was hopeless. The gun had done its job. Even if she could somehow get his heart started again, which Blake seriously doubted, he would have no kind of life left to live.

He reached across the body and touched her shoulder. "It's too late," he said, surprised by how his voice choked over the words. It wasn't his first time to witness death. He'd seen more than his share in Afghanistan, and even more in the years since. But something about this man's death touched his soul.

He stood and looked around, noting the framed photo of Ben Casey and a woman he assumed was his wife, obviously taken before the cancer—when she was healthy and vibrant. Her photo was displayed in several places and he could tell Ben had been thinking of his wife quite frequently.

Blake knew the pain of losing someone he'd been ready to marry and build a life with. How much more would it hurt to lose someone with whom you'd already spent a lifetime? He spotted a laptop computer on the desk half open and lifted the top. A Word document appeared, stating that Ben no longer wanted to remain on this earth without his beloved wife. A suicide note.

But he shook away those feelings of all he'd lost and tried to examine the room with an investigator's eye. Had the door been ajar because he'd wanted someone to find him? Or because someone hadn't locked it when they'd fled after killing the man?

Blake knelt beside the gun on the floor. The angle appeared to be correct for a self-inflicted shot to the head. But he looked at the man's hands and realized they were wrongly positioned. They were by his side in a way that said they hadn't been raised when the shot had occurred. He picked up and examined each of the man's hands. No powder burns, no gun residue.

"What is it?" Holly asked, tears welling in her eyes.

He repositioned the hands as he'd found them. "He wasn't holding the gun when it went off."

She gasped. "Are you sure?"

"Absolutely. There's no powder burns on either hand and no smell of gun residue." He locked eyes with her. "Someone staged this to look like a suicide, but it wasn't. Ben Casey was murdered."

Holly shuddered in the darkness of the minivan; Blake's words still haunted her. Why would anyone kill Mr. Casey? Was the drug ring tying up loose ends? Had Ben had a change of heart after hearing about the kids? He'd seemed genuinely distressed when he'd learned how the chemicals were being used. Had he approached them? Told them he wouldn't look the other way anymore? She could imagine him doing such a thing. Then again, perhaps their words hadn't affected him at all. Maybe he'd simply been too far in to do anything but comply.

Blake seemed certain he hadn't killed himself and she trusted his opinion. But who else would believe it? A grief-stricken widower lonely and pining for his wife. Someone had gone to great lengths to make it look like he'd taken his own life, even taking the time to type a suicide note.

"If you could tell it wasn't a suicide, won't the police be able to tell, as well?"

"What police, Holly? Chief Waggoner has been covering for Mason for years. For all I know, he ordered Mason to kill that man. Besides, remember he told me they had the coroner in their pocket? Someone made sure this looked like a suicide, so I doubt it will be investigated as anything but that."

She sighed. "I suppose you're right. If they could make Jimmy's death look like a work-related incident, they can certainly convince people that Mr. Casey took his own life. He'd been depressed for weeks."

"But it does make me wonder. Why kill him if he was working for them? Are they tying up loose ends now that they know the DEA is sniffing around?"

"And we're the loosest of all the loose ends, aren't we?"

He only nodded. It seemed redundant to repeat it. They both knew their situation was dire.

EIGHT

The phone in his pocket buzzed and Blake pulled it out. He didn't recognize the number, but he still thought they should answer it.

He gave Holly a distressed glance then pushed the button to answer it. "Hello?"

"Blake. Oh good, it's you. This is Elizabeth Banks calling."

He raised an eyebrow at Holly and put the call on speaker. "Mayor Banks? This is a nice surprise. I thought Chief Waggoner had you arrested."

"Yes, he did, and he locked me and Stephen in a cell in the police station. However, I have more friends than he knows. An officer who is loyal to my administration let us out and sneaked us out of the precinct. I imagine they've discovered we're gone by now and will be searching the streets, so you and Holly be extra careful, too."

"We will."

"I'm calling because I was able to get in touch with my friend Alex Milton, the one who owns the private plane? He's agreed to fly us out of Northshore. There's plenty of room for you and Holly."

"That's great news."

"Thank you, Mayor," Holly said.

"We'll be taking off in an hour at the airfield. Do you know where that is?"

"Yes," Holly said. "I know it. We'll be there."

"Wonderful. I'll see you both there."

She clicked off and Blake hit the button to end the call. He looked at her and saw excitement and hope bubbling in her face.

"We're going to make it," she said, sliding across the seat to give him a hug. "We're finally going to make it."

He tried to curb his enthusiasm, but the truth was that he, too, was excited at the news. Although he wished he could have an opportunity to question Sherri Livingston and try once more to discover the location of the manufacturing plant, he knew the best thing to do was to get to safety.

He put the minivan into gear and headed for the airfield.

They were finally getting out.

Holly couldn't believe the nightmare was almost over. She closed her eyes and willed herself to calm down. She knew better than to get her hopes up, but this time it seemed like a done deal.

Thank You, Lord, for seeing us through this.

The gratitude presented itself without her even realizing it and it surprised her. She did believe God had been with them throughout this ordeal and had kept them safe. Nothing else could account for the close calls they'd had. She thought about what Blake had said about letting God handle her burdens. She wanted the kind of healing he'd experienced. She closed her eyes and breathed deeply. It was time for her to let go of the anger and bitterness she'd been clinging to for the past year.

She opened her eyes and glanced at Blake. What was that verse about God repaying what the locusts ate? God was already repaying her in the form of Blake. Was he her second chance at love? She felt certain he was, but was she ready to put aside her fears for his safety and put her full trust in God? She took one more deep, fortifying breath. She thought she was.

She spotted the sign for the airfield and her heart quickened. It was really happening.

Her excitement quickly waned when Blake turned off onto a dirt road before they reached the entrance for the airfield. "What's going on?" Holly asked.

"Just being cautious. Mason has surprised us before."

He pulled over and grabbed a pair of binoculars he'd found in the cabin. He quickly got out, stood on the rear bumper and aimed the binoculars toward the airstrip. Holly realized he'd parked behind a line of trees so they couldn't be seen. It hadn't even occurred to her that this could be a trap—she was thankful again Blake was with her.

"What do you see?" she asked as she climbed out and stood at the side of the vehicle.

He reached for her hand and lifted her onto the bumper, where she had a view through the trees. The mayor and Stephen stood together by the plane. She also spotted another man with them. "Is that the pilot, do you think?"

He lowered the binoculars. "No, that's Lenny Mc-Daniels. He must have been the friend the mayor mentioned helped her get out of the jail. The pilot may be inside the plane doing preflight checks."

He handed her the binoculars and she looked through them. She could see their faces clearly and recognized Officer McDaniels from the coffee shop. Having him on their side was good news. "He must have realized what you said about Mason was true."

Blake nodded. "Which means he's one more person who can attest to the corruption of the NPD. He might know something about the drug ring even if he doesn't realize he knows it." He jumped down. "Let's get over there. I can't wait to question him."

He held up his hand to help her down and she took it. He pulled her to him and she wrapped her arms around his neck, lingering as he held her and marveling at his powerful build. She burrowed her head into his shoulder and soaked in the feel of him. After a moment, he tightened his arms around her.

"Thank you, Blake," she whispered. "I wouldn't have made it through this without you."

She lifted her head and looked at him. He gazed at her for a long moment then kissed her, his touch whisper-soft but full of hope for more. And she knew that was just what she wanted from him—more.

Blake's heart was still thumping in his ears when he pulled the minivan into the airfield and up to the plane.

The group assembled there turned as they approached and, once they realized it was them, smiled and waved. He imagined they were all on edge, like he was, anticipating an attack, although he thought Mayor Banks looked surprisingly cool as she approached them. He supposed she might simply be good at hiding her true feelings—it seemed a good skill for a politician to have.

"You made it. Wonderful!" She gave Blake a firm handshake and Holly a hug.

She led them back to the group. "You remember Stephen. And I'm certain, Blake, you know Officer McDaniels."

McDaniels reached out to shake Blake's hand. "I owe you both an apology. Everything you told me about Mason and the chief was true. I'm glad you're safe."

"I understand," Holly said. "They had me fooled, as well."

"And I underestimated you, too, Blake. The mayor told me you've been working undercover with the DEA. I confess I had my doubts about you. Now it all makes sense."

"I'd like to talk to you more in depth on the plane."

"And speaking of the plane, the pilot, Alex, is already inside. I think we should all board, as well."

"I agree," Blake said.

Holly slipped her hand into his and he led her up the steps and into the plane. He shook Alex's hand and thanked him for his assistance as Holly found a seat. He slid in beside her.

Mayor Banks turned to Stephen at the door. "I left my bag in the car. Will you please go back and retrieve it?"

Stephen nodded and headed down the steps. Blake saw him through the window and wished for him to hurry. He was ready to be in the air and on his way out of Northshore. He had an added incentive to get out now. He needed to get Holly to safety and he was looking forward to whatever the future held with her.

Suddenly something grabbed his attention through the window. A black SUV screeched to a halt and five men dressed all in black, wearing riot masks and carrying rifles, hopped out. He heard their shouts to stop and saw Stephen at the car turn and raise his hands in surrender. It didn't help. One of them raised their gun and fired. Stephen slumped to the ground.

Mayor Banks rushed to the front of the plane. "We need to take off now, Alex."

Blake leaped to his feet and was glad to see McDaniels did, as well, gun ready. "Close the door," Blake hollered and since there was no automatic stair lift, McDaniels grabbed the stairs to pull them up. As he did, the masked men began firing at the plane.

McDaniels grunted and the stairs slipped from his hand. He slumped over and Blake realized he'd been hit. His heart hammered as the men kept firing. Nothing had ever sounded as lovely as the sound of the engines firing...but he still had to get those stairs pulled up. Blake leaned over McDaniels and grabbed the lever, yanking it toward him, and the steps swept up as the plane began moving.

Blake smelled the acrid odor of gasoline and knew they'd hit the fuel line. And they were still steadily fir-

ing holes into the fuselage. They weren't going anywhere.

Another round of gunfire and Blake heard glass
breaking. The plane began to speed up.

He glanced back and saw Holly had run to the other
side of the plane and taken cover behind a seat, as had
Mayor Banks. Her cool demeanor had faded and fear
shone in her eyes.

"It was a trap," she whispered, and Blake couldn't
disagree.

He suspected Chief Waggoner had allowed McDaniels to sneak her out of the precinct so he could gather
all his enemies into one place and make it easier to take
them all down.

He crawled to his feet and ran into the cockpit. Alex
was slumped over the controls in the pilot's seat so he
slid into the copilot's seat. He didn't have any experience flying and doubted they would be able to take
off even if he could with the bullet holes the plane had
sustained. But he did need to slow the plane down so
they could get off. If Mason and his goons caught up
to them and they were still on the grounded plane, they
would be sitting targets.

He hit the brakes and brought the plane to a skid-
ding stop on the tarmac. Once stopped, he hurried out
and pushed open the stairs, then motioned for Holly and
Mayor Banks to hurry out.

"I'm afraid I'm not going to be able to run," Mayor
Banks said, her voice faltering. Blake noticed her face
was pale. She was holding her stomach and he noticed

a blood circle forming around her hand. She was bleeding badly.

Holly moved forward to help her, but she shook her head. "No, you have to go."

"We're not leaving you," Holly insisted.

"I can't run. If you stay, you won't be able to do anything to help me and you'll both be killed. You must go. Save yourself and take care of Holly. Get her out safely."

He hated to leave her, but knew she was right. They could do nothing to help her.

"Thank you for your help, Mayor."

She grabbed his hand before he could stand. "Take him down, Blake. Don't you let them get away with this."

He nodded, determination steeling his voice. He'd watched too many people die already and he was sick of it. "I will," he vowed, then stood and followed Holly down the steps.

"Head for the trees," Blake shouted and Holly complied. In fact, he had a hard time keeping up with her with his sore ankle.

He ran as best he could, checking behind him, and saw the SUV heading their way and the gunmen hopping out.

"There they are!" one of them shouted as the men ran after them.

Blake was sure Mason was one of the shooters behind the riot masks.

Holly slid and fell, hitting the ground face-first.

Blake pulled her to her feet. They had to keep going no matter what. Stopping wasn't an option.

Holly's knee was screaming after her fall, but she barreled through it. She felt tension pour off Blake as he ran beside her and she could hear his heavy breathing as he ran.

"This way," he commanded and she did as he said. She hoped he had a plan because there was no way they could outrun bullets if Mason got close enough to start firing.

She ran behind a tree and Blake pulled her to a stop and motioned for her to remain silent. He crouched behind the trunk and peeked around it. Holly peeked, too, and spotted one of the men approaching, his gun raised as he looked around the area.

Blake tensed, then rushed him as he got close and grabbed the rifle. The gun went off and Holly fell backward, stunned by the noise it made. The two men struggled and the rifle slipped through their hands and fell to the ground. The man lunged for it, but Blake grabbed him and threw him down, pulling off his mask and tossing it, confirming to Holly that it was Mason behind the mask.

Anger bit at her again at how Mason had ruined her life. He'd killed Jimmy. She was certain of that. He'd made her a target and forced her to run for her life. Now he'd murdered people who were trying to help her.

Rage filled her. She was done running.

While Blake struggle hand-to-hand with Mason, Holly moved past them and swooped up the rifle. The weight of the cold metal in her hands empowered her with control of the situation. She fired off a round to get their attention and both men stopped struggling and spun around to face her.

Mason's face reddened with anger and his eyes narrowed. "Give. That. Back."

She aimed the barrel at him. "Not a chance."

Blake leaped to his feet and grabbed Mason by the collar, pulling him upright. "Get up," he commanded.

Mason staggered to his feet. He sneered at her. "You won't fire that thing, Holly. You don't have it in you to kill anyone."

"You murdered my husband," she said, surprised at how her voice cracked. "And you just killed all those people on the plane. Jimmy taught me how to shoot. So, if I were you, Mason, I wouldn't second-guess what I am capable of." She heard the way her tone turned hard as she spoke and at that moment was unsure how much it would bother her to shoot him. But Blake's hand on her shoulder pressed into her, pulling her back from that dark place.

"You're not a killer, Holly," his gentle voice insisted. He pulled the gun from her hands and pointed it at Mason. "But *I will* shoot you, and not lose a moment's sleep over it."

Mason sneered at them again, but conceded and raised his hands over his head.

Holly stayed behind Blake as he marched Mason back through the field toward the plane and Mason's waiting crew.

"Holly, get down on the ground. Stay there until I tell you differently."

She lay down and studied the situation. She counted four men present around the SUV. They'd removed their riot masks, and Holly recognized each one by their faces, but also from their names in Jimmy's journal. He'd known they were corrupt cops.

"Drop your weapons!" Blake called and they all turned toward him, raising their guns. Blake stayed behind Mason, but made it clear he would shoot Mason if they didn't do what he commanded.

"Do what he says," Mason commanded.

The men reluctantly did so.

"Kick them out of the way," Blake told them and again they complied. "Now move toward the plane. Go!" They hurried over, hands raised and defeat on their faces. "Where are the keys to the SUV? Who has them?"

"In my pocket," Mason said shortly, and only the resignation in his voice surprised Holly. Of course he held on to the keys. Mason wouldn't have given up control of anything, including letting his men take off without him.

Blake dug into Mason's pocket and retrieved the keys, holding them out to Holly. "Take them. Start the car."

She saw what he was thinking. They were going to use Mason's vehicle to make their escape. She jumped up and grabbed the keys, then ran for the SUV. On the tarmac, she noticed the bodies of Mayor Banks, Stephen and the pilot. Mason's men had obviously removed them from the plane. A wave of sadness filled her at the sight and she wondered how she ever believed anything Mason or the chief told her. She crawled into the SUV and slid in the key, started it up, and guided it closer to where Blake had moved Mason with his men. He was watching them bind each other's hands, and checking the zip-ties.

Her heart was racing as he back-stepped to the vehicle and then hopped inside. "Punch it," he told her and she gladly took off, speeding away from the carnage Mason and his men had caused. She felt Blake start to relax as she turned out of the airfield.

"What do we do now?" she asked him.

"We play the only card we have left," he told her. "We have to find Sherri Livingston and pray she knows where the manufacturing plant is located."

Holly agreed and headed for the hospital. She prayed they could find Sherri and she could provide the answers they needed.

Holly remembered the day she'd approached Sherri about the invoice that had landed in her inbox by accident. As the charge nurse, her department was responsible for the supplies they used. She'd been relieved when Sherri had assured her it was a billing error. She'd even laughed about having a warehouse full of cleaning supplies. Holly had been glad to hear it.

Holly replayed in her mind the events of that day. Sherri had seemed nervous when Holly had approached her, just after receiving a notice from the Social Security Office that there'd been a review of Jimmy's benefits. She'd spent three hours on the phone to correct it then cried for another two hours missing him and dealing with the fallout of his death. She remembered feeling dismayed at yet another problem she'd had to deal with, so she'd been relieved when Sherri had assured her it was a billing error.

Now, she fumed. She should have noticed the worry on Sherri's face and the way her hands had shaken, but she hadn't thought much about it at the time. She'd been too wrapped up in her own problems to worry about someone else's. Maybe that's what happened to Ben. It burned her up that grief had made it so easy to deceive her, and maybe the old widower, too.

She spotted Sherri exiting the hospital. Holly reached for the door, ready to jump out and confront her, but Blake touched her shoulder, gently calling her back.

"I can see you're worked up and ready to fight, but this is our last chance to get answers. So we have to be smart. We can't scare her off. We need to impress on her the danger she's in. Can you do that?"

She took a deep, fortifying breath then let it out slowly. Of course he was right. She'd almost blown it by flying off the handle. She looked at him and nodded. "I understand."

"Our first goal is to find out exactly how involved she is. Is she a willing participant who knows what she's doing or someone Mason intimidated into doing what he told her? How well do you know her?"

Holly sighed. "I don't, really. I know who she is and we see each other around the hospital, but we don't have a personal relationship. I noticed a picture on her desk of a little girl. She's a mother."

"Well, I would hate to use her child against her, but I guarantee Mason has made that threat to her."

"How will we convince her to talk to us if he's threatened her daughter?"

"By making sure she knows we're her only hope of protecting her daughter. She has to understand that Mason is the enemy."

They got out and approached Sherri as she headed for her car. When Holly called her name, Sherri turned and her eyes widened. "Holly?" She glanced around, her expression conveying hope that someone would be nearby to help her. "What are you doing here? I heard you'd been abducted. It's all over the hospital. Security is even insisting we don't walk to our cars alone."

"I guess you're wishing you'd listened to that advice, aren't you?" Blake suggested.

"But you didn't worry because you knew I hadn't been abducted, didn't you, Sherri? You knew that Mason tried to kill me and I was running for my life."

Her eyes widened again and she backed up against her car. "I don't know what you're talking about. Someone tried to kill you?"

Holly couldn't believe the gall of the woman, denying her involvement.

"I'm glad you're safe, but I really have to go." She opened her car door, but Blake shut it again and stood in front of it. "Let me go."

"You're not going anywhere until you tell us what we need to know."

"And what's that?"

"Where they're manufacturing the drugs."

"I have no idea what you're talking about." She jutted her chin, her tone impertinent. "Now I really have to go."

"Do you know what they're doing with those chemicals, Sherri? They're using them to manufacture drugs that they hand out to *kids*. Children are dying! And you're complicit in their deaths. Not to mention the deaths of everyone else Mason has murdered."

She gasped, shocked. "Murdered? Who—?"

"Mayor Banks and two members of her staff. Officer Lenny McDaniels. Alex Milton. Mr. Casey from the loading dock."

"I—I heard Mr. Casey committed suicide. He was distraught after his wife's death."

Blake spoke through clenched teeth, "Mason tried to make it look like a suicide, but he was definitely murdered. They're tying up loose ends, Sherri. It won't be long before they'll get around to killing you, too."

She jutted that chin again. "Mason wouldn't do that."

"But Mason isn't the one in charge, is he? He's taking orders from someone who doesn't care a lick about you. Let's face it. You messed up by letting Holly see that invoice. If Mason had been able to complete the job of killing Holly, I'm certain you would have been his next target."

She clutched her bag tighter and Holly could see Blake was getting through to her. She knew Sherri wasn't to blame for that. Someone in the mailroom messed up and sent it to Holly by mistake, but she felt certain Mason blamed Sherri for the mix-up.

"I can protect you," he said. "I have friends with the DEA. They can work out some kind of witness protection for you."

Holly saw her struggling with her decision and then her face hardened. "You can't even get yourselves out of this town. Why would I believe you can protect me?"

"Because we're your only hope."

Holly was surprised by the intensity of the truth in his words.

Sherri heard it, too, because she pulled a hand through her hair and indecision returned to her face.

In that moment Holly knew that Sherri wasn't comfortable being a part of this operation. She was either lured by the money or maybe the attention of Mason, or he'd threatened her from day one. Either way, Holly knew the look of a person who'd seen Mason's dark side.

Finally, Sherri sighed and put her hands over her face. When she looked back up, resignation was written across it. "I don't know how much help I can be to you. I don't know where the plant is. Mason kept it supersecret from me. He said he had to be careful because someone already discovered its location once before."

"Who was that?" Blake asked.

Sherri glanced at her. "It was your husband. Mason said he followed him there one night. That's when they knew they had to kill him, because he was about to jeopardize their operation."

Holly's stomach tightened. She could imagine Jimmy tracking Mason's movements and following him covertly. To think he'd been so close to uncovering a major drug operation and she'd never known. Anger bit at her again toward Mason and whoever he was working for.

"Who's the guy in charge?" she asked Sherri.

The young woman shook her head. "I don't know."

Holly was frustrated by her lack of information. "How can you not know who you work for?"

"I only deal with Mason. He's the one who tells me what shipments to conceal and what paperwork needs to disappear. At first, it seemed harmless. By the time I realized what I was involved in, it was too late to get out."

"I need you to think, Sherri," Blake said, pressing her for more info. "Did Mason ever say anything that would indicate who was in charge? You may not have even realized it at the time."

But tears were already sliding down her face and Holly could see she was fast losing her composure. "I don't know. I just don't know. He would never tell me. He only threatened me, telling me that he worked for powerful men." She wiped away tears with the back of her hand. "I have a daughter. She depends on me. He said he would kill her if I didn't do what he said. At first, I was blown away by the money. I'm a single mother and it really helped, but soon he was wanting me to do more and more. When I protested, he threatened my family and said I was in too deep."

"Thank you for your honesty, Sherri. Your daughter would be proud of you."

A tear slid down her cheek but she pushed it away and straightened. "I have to leave," she said, trying to push Blake away from her car.

"Wait, you're leaving? Where are you going?"

"I can't be around you. If Mason finds out I even talked to you, he will kill me."

Blake stepped forward. "I can't protect you if you don't come with us."

"No, I can't. I have to go pick up my daughter. I have to get her somewhere safe."

Blake touched her arm to try to calm her down. "It's okay. It's okay. But get somewhere safe, Sherri, because things are about to go south for Mason and his friends."

She looked at him, her eyes wide with fear. "I understand."

She got into her car and started the engine, then roared away.

Holly watched Sherri leave and felt their last bit of hope leave with her. "What do we do now?" she asked Blake, but he didn't look nearly as downtrodden as she felt.

"Sherri just gave us a clue as to where the drug plant is located. She said Jimmy followed Mason there the night before he died."

He hurried to the car and retrieved the journal. He flipped through it to the back and read the last words her husband had recorded.

"'Followed Mason a half mile down the causeway, where he turned off and stopped in front of an old repair shop. He remained for only ten minutes then left, returning to his own home for the night. Not sure of his reasons for going there, but it might be worth checking out tomorrow after my shift.'"

Tears were on Holly's face when Blake finished reading the passage. Jimmy had never completed that shift. He'd been murdered that very night. Was it because of what he'd seen at that repair shop?

"I remember seeing this place he's talking about on the map of the town, but it didn't raise any red flags for me at the time. It's an established business that's been in operation for over twenty years, according to city records. We should check it out."

She agreed and they headed for the car. She stopped and turned to him when the phone rang. He glanced at the screen and a frown creased his forehead.

"What's the matter?"

"It's Mayor Banks's cell phone number." He pressed the answer button and put the phone to his ear.

The frown deepened.

"Holly? Is that you? You never returned my call," the voice on the other end said. Blake knew the chief's voice immediately, but why was he calling from the mayor's phone and why was he asking for Holly?

"What do you want with her?" Blake asked, and the chief's voice changed from smooth and amicable to hard as a rock.

"Blake, let's end this nonsense. Turn yourself in and accept your consequences. Holly shouldn't be a part of this."

"I didn't make her a part of this," he reminded the chief. "Mason did."

"As I've already told Holly, I can handle Mason."

His heart sank. Holly had been talking to Chief Waggoner behind his back. He turned to her. Her eyes were wide with curiosity. Anger pulsed through him. "You've done an awesome job of controlling him so far. I think he's doing just what you've instructed him to do."

"Be practical, Blake. There's no way out. This is my town, and your friends at the DEA can't change that."

Blake hated to think he was right. If he couldn't find the manufacturing plant, Matt and the DEA would not be able to enter. This new lead had promise, but now his head was spinning with the idea that Holly had betrayed him.

"Don't underestimate me," he said before hitting the off button on the phone.

Holly was suddenly beside him. "That was Chief Waggoner? What did he say?"

He fisted his hands to keep them from shaking as anger rolled through him like a freight train. He locked eyes with her. "Have you been talking to him behind my back?"

Her mouth dropped open at his angry accusation. "No, of course not. He called the night you were hurt and I did speak with him, but I wasn't trying to hide it."

"What did he want?"

She didn't flinch as she responded to him. "He wanted me to turn you in. He said I could go back to my normal life if I handed you over to him. I told him no."

Her reassurance should have made him feel better, but it didn't. Now he was suddenly questioning everything, like why her husband had never told her about his investigation or why she hadn't noticed anything fishy about the invoice that had been routed to her in error. But mostly, he was wondering if he needed to watch his back. Miranda hadn't hesitated to turn on her friends for a little bit of money. What, he wondered, was Holly's price?

As he got into the SUV, he felt like beating his hand against the steering column, but refrained. He wouldn't be a fool again, but had he fallen for another woman who wasn't what she seemed? It was Miranda all over again. Was she playing him for a fool? He glanced at her and felt his heart clench. He couldn't believe it…but then, he hadn't been able to believe in Miranda, either.

He lifted a silent prayer. *Lord, have I messed up again?* Pastor Dave had helped him to realize that he'd not been listening to God when he was involved with Miranda. He'd claimed to be a good, Christian man who loved the Lord, but it hadn't been reflected in his life. If he'd been focusing on the Lord instead of on his own feelings, he might have seen Miranda for what she really was.

He sighed. That was all in the past. He'd mourned his loss with her and moved on…or so he thought. But each glance at the dark-haired beauty beside him filled him with suspicion. How could he even trust what he felt for her? How could he be sure he could trust her? He didn't trust himself and that was the problem. He couldn't trust his own judgment anymore when it came to women. He saw deceit everywhere he looked.

He pulled in a deep, calming breath and felt the peace of the Lord settle over him. He didn't have to trust in Holly. He only had to trust in what God had given him and he was trying, really trying. But that nagging doubt kept pushing its way to the front of his mind.

He pulled out the cell phone and hit the redial button. Matt answered a moment later.

"I may have the location of the manufacturing plant. We're on our way there now."

"I'll have satellite imagery confirm this so I need those coordinates when you arrive. While they're doing that, I'll work up a plan to get you both out of there."

Blake nodded and said tersely, "The sooner the better."

Holly looked at him as he hung up with Matt. "How long will it take the DEA to act?"

"They'll have to confirm the location before the higher-ups will approve breaching the town's lockdown. Once that's done, they'll put together a team to come in. Chief Waggoner will have no choice but to allow them in."

She sighed. "Legally, he might be obligated, but he's a criminal. Who's to say he won't just start shooting when they try to cross the bridge?"

Blake nodded. "He might, but I can guarantee the DEA has men trained to face situations like this. Matt is a former Ranger and I know for certain he's dealt with men like Chief Waggoner before. He'll try negotiating first, but if that doesn't work, he won't just give up." He didn't add that Matt also wouldn't give up on him. Blake knew he could depend on his friend to help him out of this mess. He wouldn't abandon him, no matter what. He could trust the Rangers above everyone else. But could he trust Holly? That was the real question.

He hated that his mind immediately went to distrust, but those nagging doubts were flooding back to him.

He was finally beginning to trust her and now this. He tried to push those doubts away. She wasn't Miranda and it wasn't fair to judge her by the same standards, but he couldn't shake the feeling.

Lord, I'm worried. Can I trust what I'm feeling for Holly?

He wanted to believe she was all she claimed to be.

The silence in the car was deafening as Blake drove. He seemed tense and distant as they headed out of town toward the old boat dock. Gone was the assured self-confidence she'd come to know in him. He seemed like a stranger beside her and she no longer felt the assurance that it was okay to reach out and touch him. She didn't like the change in him, and she knew what had caused it. Chief Waggoner's phone call.

"I wasn't keeping it from you," she insisted.

His jaw clenched. "Well, you weren't being very forthcoming with it either, were you?"

"Are you really doubting me because of a phone call?"

"No, it's more than that. There were signs and I should have seen them. Your own husband didn't trust you enough to tell you about his investigation. Plus, by your own admission, you saw that invoice and didn't do anything about it."

Tears pressed against her eyes but she blinked them back. She wouldn't cry in front of him. It hurt to have him doubt her. They were supposed to be on the same side. They were both fighting against Mason and the drug ring.

She remembered the conversation they'd had about

Miranda and how she'd betrayed him. She'd scarred him, caused him to doubt his own judgment. It hurt that he now saw her lumped in with someone who'd betrayed him.

"I don't know what I can say to change your mind about me. All I can do is assure you that it isn't true. I don't know why Jimmy kept this from me, but I suspect it was because he worried for my safety. He knew what he was doing was dangerous. And if you really want the truth then, yes, I was very briefly tempted by Chief Waggoner's offer, but I turned it down partly because I know he can't be trusted, but mainly because I could never leave you, Blake. I thought you knew me better than that after all we've been through together."

He sighed and rubbed his face then looked at her. She saw confusion cloud his blue eyes. "I thought I knew you. Now I'm not so sure."

Her heart broke at his words. She'd thought she'd finally found someone she could open her heart to and love again. But she wouldn't be with someone who didn't believe in her.

NINE

Blake pulled out his binoculars and looked around the area. Just as he'd expected, he saw the telltale signs of drug manufacturing at the repair shop—blacked-out windows, burned grassy areas and a large venting system on the far wall.

"They're cooking something in there," Blake said then realized no one was there to hear him. Holly was still sulking in the SUV, well out of earshot. Maybe it was for the best. She probably needed time to cool off. So did he.

He took out his cell phone and called Matt, giving him the exact coordinates for the satellite using an app he'd downloaded.

"Be sure to wave at the camera," Matt joked, but Blake knew he was nervous. He was having a difficult time dealing with the men responsible for approving this mission. He needed this satellite imagery to return something helpful. "And tell Holly I said not to worry. I can't wait to meet the woman who's brought you back to life again."

Blake gave a weary sigh. "Well…"

"What happened? I thought you said she was terrific."

"I thought she was."

"Talk to me, Blake. Something happened in the last few hours to change your mind about her. I want to know what it was."

"It was nothing. Okay, it was something. I found out that Holly has been talking to Chief Waggoner and I didn't know it." Blake pressed his fingers against the bridge of his nose. "She says she wasn't trying to keep it from me. I don't know. I want to trust her."

"Then trust her."

"What if she's playing me? What if I'm seeing only what I want to see, Matt? I've got to tell you, I've fallen for this gal hard. What am I going to do if she's not who she says she is?"

Matt's tone grew calm but serious. "You're going to pick yourself back up again and you're going to keep going. It's all you can do. Look, Blake, I don't know everything that happened between you and Miranda, but only God can ever really know a person's heart. Are you listening to His guidance or your own?"

Blake turned and stared at Holly, who was slumped in the seat, arms folded and a hurt expression on her face. He felt an overwhelming sense of love for her. But it had happened so fast and he just wasn't sure.

He had been trying to keep his ear attuned to the Lord's words and each prayer he prayed seemed to lead him right back to Holly. He had to admit, he felt at home with her in a way that shouldn't make any sense since they'd been running for their lives the entire time he'd known her. But he'd seen her under pressure and that kind of intensity always brought true character to light. So far, he hadn't seen anything he didn't like. It was the worry and anxiousness and trying to read between the lines of her words that exhausted him and made him all tense. It was a similar feeling he'd had when he'd heard something about Miranda. He hadn't had to wonder if it was true. He'd known it was. Miranda hadn't hidden her desires for wealth and money and a better lifestyle. He'd only downplayed them because he'd wanted to fit her into the model for his picture-perfect life.

"Listen," Matt continued. "It's not like you have to make a decision today. We'll get you two out and you can spend a few weeks or months really getting to know her before you decide you're in love with her."

But that was the rub, wasn't it? He already was in love with her. It had happened without his consent. She'd stolen his heart. She already had the power to devastate him and he'd handed it to her without even a struggle.

"Show me your hands now!" a voice shouted.

Blake spun around and saw a group of men emerge from the woods, weapons raised as they surrounded Blake.

"Who are you?" one of them asked. "What are you doing here?"

"Drop the phone," another demanded and Blake dropped it to the ground, leaving the line open for Matt to hear what was happening.

Holly jumped from the SUV and started to run, but

one of the men grabbed her and dragged her toward Blake. His mind shot off a slew of different ways he would hurt the man if he harmed Holly. But the next instant had him wondering if she'd used the time while he was on the phone with Matt to alert the people inside that they were out there.

The man patted Blake down and pulled out his gun, slipping it into his own belt. "Call the boss, tell him we found the guy and girl he was looking for sneaking around the shop." He looked at Blake and shook his head. "You're both in for it now. The boss will want to meet with you both personally right before he kills you."

Blake glanced at Holly and saw fear in her face. Fear that their time had just run out.

All of his anger and rage burst through him as a vehicle skidded to a stop and Mason jumped out. Blake wasn't surprised he'd gotten free of the zip-tie cuff where they'd left him. He was resourceful, but this man had tried to take everything from him and had taken everything from Holly.

He knew the truth as Mason confronted him. He wanted his life back. He wanted to be out of this nightmare and back on his acreage, rocking on his back porch and watching the sun set. And he knew he wanted Holly by his side. No use denying it any longer. He had fallen for her. He could picture a life with her and it was a life that he wanted. He didn't want to doubt anymore. He didn't want to spend the rest of his life waiting for the other shoe to drop. She could wound him and she might, but he couldn't continue living this way.

Mason threw a punch and Blake swerved, missing

it then returning with a fist to his gut. He rebounded, grabbing Blake's arm and twisting it. Pain ripped through that shoulder. Mason knew just how to hurt him and he fought dirty. He had no honor. He was no better than the injustice Blake had fought overseas.

Mason shoved him toward the SUV and Blake hit it hard, jamming his shoulder again.

"What should we do with her?" one of the men asked, pulling Holly closer.

"Tie their hands and put them in the car. The boss will want to see them."

Blake's gut clenched. They were finally going to find out who was the person behind Mason's reign of terror. And it was probably the last discovery either of them would ever make.

Mason and his goons drove them the short distance to the repair shop and stopped in front. As they were pulled from the vehicle and led through the building, Holly smelled the stench of chemicals cooking and spotted people in sealed-up areas wearing special clothing. They were cooking up poison to distribute to kids. She could think of nothing more vile.

The gun at her back was cold and hard as Mason jabbed her with it, prodding her along. She walked, Blake at her side. He still seemed distant and as cold as the steel frame of the shop. At this moment, she felt utterly alone and frightened. Holly couldn't resist staring up at the clear blue sky outside the high windows. Light filtered in and hit the back of Blake's neck, illuminating the scar jutting out from his shirt. She realized he might be too jaded to ever trust her. *Lord, please bend his heart to mine.* But she wasn't alone and she knew that now. God was with her and would see her through this nightmare even if Blake had left her emotionally.

Mason pushed past her and reached for a large door with a padlock on the outside. He slid it open then motioned them inside. Blake walked in, his gaze never leaving Mason's face and his eyes blazing. Holly followed him, noticing how much darker it was inside this room. She glanced around and saw that there were no windows in here.

"Enjoy your last few minutes." Mason sneered before pulling on the door. It slid shut then clanked as it latched. She heard the sounds of Mason snapping the padlock into place, locking them inside.

Blake felt along the walls and the door, looking for some weakness to exploit. They had to get out of this room if they were to have any chance of survival. He knew Matt was working on a plan to get them out, but he didn't know if it would be in time.

He didn't have to think long to know what the likely plan was. The DEA was probably scrambling to push through the barricades and mobilizing a breach. Mason's boss probably saw Blake and Holly as bargaining chips to keep them off his back while he closed down shop in Northshore.

That was okay. He didn't mind being used as a pawn if it meant he got a few more hours to breathe and figure out a means of escape.

Holly slid to the floor. He could tell she was weary

and fearful, but more than that he felt the tension between them. He wanted to reassure her that he believed
her, that he trusted her, and he did…at least, he was trying. But he'd been trained to watch for subterfuge and
he'd honed his skills in that area over the past twelve
months.

Even now, part of him wondered if this wasn't all
a ploy. Was she working with Mason and they'd been
locked in this room to give her an opportunity to ferret out what the DEA knew about the operation? Why
hadn't they been killed on the spot? Mason had tried
time and time again and had failed to kill Holly. Was it
because he wasn't really trying? It hadn't felt that way
during each attempt. It had felt real and Holly's fear
had seemed real.

Why do I do this to myself, Lord?

It was fear rearing its ugly head. He pushed it back.
He'd faced down bullets and armed gunmen, mortar
rounds and automatic weapons, and managed to keep
fear under control. Now it was threatening to rule his
life again. He thought back on the words Pastor Dave
had spoken to him, words that hadn't found their mark
until just now.

Holly chuckled and shook her head.

"What's so funny?"

"You. We're facing death and yet you still can't stop
thinking about that phone call. I'm sitting here locked
up with you and you still don't trust me. What do you
think, Blake, that I'm some mole sent in here by Mason's boss to ferret out what the DEA knows about their
operation? I'm not. I was never involved with Mason,

Chief Waggoner or the drug ring. We're on the same side."

He stared at her then rubbed sweat from his face. "I want to believe that."

"Then believe it."

"Holly, you know—"

"I know, your fiancée betrayed you and now you don't know whether or not you can trust anyone ever again." She sighed wearily then her voice grew firm. "Get over it."

"Excuse me?"

"We're fighting for our lives here, Blake, and you're focusing on something that doesn't matter at all."

"That's a little harsh, Holly."

"No, it isn't, because these may very well be my last moments on earth and I want to spend them with you, Blake. I know it's terrifying to put your heart out there, but life is messy and love doesn't come with a guarantee. All we can do is listen to God, try to do the best we can and let Him pick up the pieces when we fall. You told me that, remember? Well, it's true. Control is a fantasy. And you're over there obsessing about something that doesn't make a lick of difference."

"Really? Whether or not I can trust you doesn't matter?"

"Not now. We're trapped in here, Blake, about to die, and you have to make a choice. Either take me in your arms and kiss me, or die alone knowing that I've fallen completely in love with you and I want to be with you."

The words had barely left her lips when the distinct thump, thump, thump of a helicopter filled the air.

Blake's heart soared at the sound. "It's them," Blake said. "They're here to save us."

Outside the door, he heard a commotion, footsteps running, shouts of warning and, a moment later, gunfire. He heard a loud explosion and knew it was probably the team blowing the doors off the building. He'd been part of search-and-rescue teams and knew how they worked. They would take out the men inside then sweep the building for hostages.

He started pounding on the door, shouting out to whoever was on the other side to listen. "Here! We're in here!"

After a moment Holly started banging on the door, as well. "We're locked inside!" she called.

Blake stopped when a voice from the other side of the door spoke. "Blake?"

He recognized Garrett's voice in a heartbeat. "Yes! It's us. We're locked in here."

"Stand back. I'm going to blow the door."

He grabbed Holly and pulled her back to a corner then crouched beside her. Her pulse was racing and her breathing was heavy as she knelt beside him and pressed her hands into his arm. "Everything is going to be okay," he told her. "The Rangers are here now." He took a deep breath and looked at her. "Everything is going to be fine."

She gave him a half-hearted smile then lifted her chin and stared into his eyes with a gaze that spoke volumes about her trust in him. She moved her hand to his face then placed a kiss on his mouth. It stunned him more than anything but surprised him, too. How could she trust in him after he'd doubted her? But Garrett's shout of warning came before he could respond.

He pushed Holly down, hovering over her, ready to deflect any shrapnel created by the blast. He braced for the impact and, a moment later, heard the pop of the explosion and felt heat on his back. When he looked up again, the door was hanging on one hinge. A swift kick by the man in the military gear took it down and he stepped inside and pulled off his oxygen mask to reveal his friend's familiar face.

"Let's get you both out of here."

Blake stopped to shake his hand. "I'm glad you're part of the team," he said. He trusted Garrett with his life and was glad Matt had been able to rope him into leading the assault. However, as he stepped out into the shop he saw several of the drug runners on the ground, bound and gagged, but a swift glance revealed none of them was Mason. He'd gotten away again. Even more bothersome, Blake counted only three men in assault gear—Garrett, Colton and Josh.

"What happened?" he asked. "Where's the DEA strike team?"

"In a hanger somewhere trapped by government red tape." Colton reached out and shook his hand. Josh also stepped forward and shook his hand. "We couldn't wait for them to come in any longer so we decided to make the move ourselves. Matt knew a former pilot who agreed to help out with the chopper, but Matt had to stay back and cover with the higher-ups."

He still only counted four men out of their six-man squad. "What happened to Levi?"

"Another surgery last week," Garrett said. "This time to repair a slipped disc in his back. He wanted to be here but at this point it's amazing he's still walking."

Blake nodded. "This is Holly," he said, introducing her to the group.

"Nice to meet you, Holly," Colton said, "but we'll have time for chitchat later. Right now, we have to move. Parker has that bird parked in a pasture but who knows how long he'll be able to stay there."

Holly slipped her hand into Blake's. A ripple of pleasure burst through him to know that he hadn't blown it with her, after all. He closed his hand over hers then helped her through the building, remaining close by her side as they walked. Once they were outside, he followed his friends' lead and ran toward the chopper in the clearing.

He felt Holly shudder beside him. "Keep your head low," he told Holly, to avoid the powerful wind created by the blades of the chopper. He hurried forward, Holly's hand firmly grasped in his.

He'd thought he could do this all by himself, that he didn't need anybody. Yet he'd needed God and he'd needed this woman by his side. He knew now his doubts about her had been fearfully motivated.

Seeing his friends rushing in to help him revived a feeling inside Blake that he thought he'd lost. He'd come here to hide away from his shame and sin, but instead he'd been drowning in it. He needed someone to pull him out of it just as the Rangers were doing it now. He realized that Jesus, too, had been there holding out His hand to Blake and he'd been too proud and too stubborn to reach out and take the help He offered. He would never turn away help from one of the Rangers, so why was he too proud to accept it from his Savior? He didn't know.

The big side doors were wide open and Josh hopped aboard first followed by Garrett and Colton, who then turned to grab Blake's hand and pull him up.

Holly's yank on his arm stopped him. "What about the drug ring? What about Mason?"

Blake glanced down at her then leaned close so she could hear his answer over the whirl of the chopper's blades. "We don't have the authority to take them into custody or to shut down their operation. All we can do for now is to get to safety and trust that Matt can win with diplomacy or coordinate another assault to take down the drug ring." All he knew for now was that they were safe and Mason and his friends were on the defensive. They had been exposed for who they were and what they were doing.

Blake and Holly climbed aboard.

"We're all on!" Josh yelled to the pilot. He gave the thumbs-up and moments later the chopper started to lift off.

Blake felt a flutter of relief. It was over. They were finally out of Northshore. They were safe. His arm tightened around Holly and she leaned into him. *Thank You, God.* They were finally safe.

Suddenly shots rang out and Blake heard the distinct sound of metal hitting metal. The helicopter swayed a bit but continued its lift. Colton raised his weapon to return fire but another shot sent him reeling backward.

"Colton!" Blake released Holly and turned to his friend lying on the chopper floor. Another shot rang out and Garrett went sprawling. Josh rushed to him.

"Keep going! Keep going!" Blake hollered to the pilot.

Blake knelt beside Colton and saw the bullets had hit his protective vest. He would hurt but he would be fine.

Holly screamed.

He turned and saw Mason appear just below the opening. He reached out and grabbed her leg, hanging on to the ascending chopper and yanking Holly out the door. Blake lunged, grabbing her hand before Mason could pull her out. But his grasp slipped. It wasn't strong and he was having a hard time firming it up. Holly's green eyes were wide with fear as her hand slipped through his and the chopper banked, tossing him backward. She slid from his grasp and from the chopper.

Blake shouted her name and ran to the edge, watching as she hit the ground, landing almost on top of Mason. Blake nearly leaped from the chopper before someone grabbed him and stopped him. He turned and saw Garrett holding him back.

"It's too far," he said. "You'll break a leg."

"We have to go back!" Blake yelled.

"We can't land," Garrett said. "We have to get out."

The continued sound of shots being fired brought him back to reality. They were under fire and the chopper was in danger. If they didn't go now, they might all be trapped.

He nodded, resigned that he had no choice. It was truly too late. The chopper was already in the air.

He looked down and saw Holly crawling to her feet. She didn't appear to be hurt, but she glanced up at the chopper before Mason grabbed her.

As they roared out of sight, the last image he had of her was Mason holding her at gunpoint and dragging her away.

Holly stiffened as Mason grabbed her arm and dragged her back to the repair shop.

"He left you," Mason snarled in her ear. "He left you."

She glanced up at the helicopter disappearing in the distant sky. She could still hear the distinct clomp of the rotor blades fading away. None of this had gone as planned, but she knew in her heart that Blake wouldn't have left her. His eyes had held fear as he'd grabbed for her and regret when he'd realized he couldn't hold on to her. Mason had bested them all this time.

Lord, I hope he's safe.

Her mind went directly to his safety. She'd tried so hard to keep her heart guarded, but the handsome former soldier had barreled his way into it.

She didn't know what Mason was going to do to her. Why hadn't he just shot her then and there for Blake to see? It would have been Mason's perfect revenge against them both. But he hadn't, which meant he probably wanted something more from her. Torture, perhaps. She'd seen his sadistic side and knew he could be merciless.

But she wasn't giving up. She was just biding her time, watching and waiting for an opportunity to escape his grasp. She prayed it would come. She wasn't ready to die yet. Not now when she'd finally found someone who'd opened her heart again. And she knew Blake would find a way to return for her.

He pulled her into the shop, where men were cleaning up the mess the Rangers had made when they'd burst inside. She saw everyone was unbound and was now busily cleaning up. Mason yelled out a few orders to people as he walked by. She spotted the steel door at the back, still off the hinges, and knew at least he couldn't put her in there. He led her into a back room that looked like it was once an office. It was a small enclosure with a door and a window that looked out onto the concrete floor.

He set down his rifle then pushed her into a chair and bound her hands behind it. As the ties dug into her wrists, she felt a sense of doom overcome her. This was the end for her and she still didn't have any answers to her questions. Who was behind the drug ring operating in town? And would that person also get away with murder? She thought he probably would. After all, they'd gotten away with Jimmy's murder. Who knew how many people he had on his payroll? Chief Waggoner definitely. Who else was involved?

She closed her eyes and tried to drown out the noise around her. She couldn't focus on that. If she did, it would make her sick with worry and that wasn't how she wanted to spend her last moments.

Instead she spent the time praying that God would rescue her from this situation. She didn't know if He would, but she knew no matter what happened, she wasn't alone. God was here with her. She felt the peace He provided and it kept her from losing all hope. She also found herself praying for Blake, that he would be able to finally find peace and to rebuild his life. He had so much to offer and he'd been so wounded by his fiancée's betrayals. She prayed that God would heal his heart and help him to learn to love and trust again.

"We have to go back for her," Blake shouted, but the firm hands on his shoulders told him they weren't returning. He glanced from Colton to Josh and then to Garrett. Each one of their faces showed the same determination. They wouldn't agree to go back.

"We can't take the chopper back into that," Garrett said. "We almost didn't make it out. And Parker will never take us back in until he gets this bird repaired. We took several hits."

In his heart, Blake knew they were right. They'd done the only thing they could do, but it didn't make him feel any better. The memory of the fear on Holly's face as she'd slipped through his hands haunted him. He'd let her down, both before and after they'd escaped from Mason. He should never have doubted her.

Either take me in your arms and kiss me, or die alone knowing that I've fallen completely in love with you and I want to be with you.

Once they landed, he leaped from the chopper and hurried toward the hanger.

"Where are you going?" Josh demanded, following behind him.

"I'm going back to get her. I left her there," Blake said. "I left her."

"You didn't leave her. We had to get out or we would all have been captured."

"Well, I'm going back for her." He had no idea yet how he would accomplish that, but he was going. He wouldn't leave her to face Mason alone.

Colton stepped in front of him. "We just got you out of that town and now you're all fired up to go back in. How will you get out next time?"

Blake stopped and turned to them, a frown forming on his face. Was his team really saying they wouldn't help him again? It felt wrong and odd. They'd always had his back and he theirs.

Matt exited the hanger door and met him. "You made it!" He glanced around. "Where's Holly?"

"She slipped through my hands," Blake told him.

Colton rushed to explain. "Blake, you know we're there for you. What I meant to say was that it's too risky to go back in without a plan to get out. We won't be able to come back in for you because we'll be with you."

He glanced around at their nodding heads. His friends—Josh, Colton and Garrett, even Matt. He depended on them and they were always there. He needed them now more than ever.

"I can't leave her," he told them, his voice choking with emotion. "He'll kill her." Suddenly he knew there was no doubt left in his mind about her. She wasn't a mole for Mason. She was in trouble and he would do whatever he had to do to get her back.

"He won't," Garrett stated firmly. "We'll stop them."

He looked at Matt. "This isn't just about stopping a drug ring for me anymore."

Matt nodded and sighed. "I know that."

"I love her."

Colton huffed. "No kidding." He slapped Blake on the back. "Now let's go work out a plan to rescue your lady."

As they walked into the hanger, Blake thought about the look of terror on Holly's face as they'd flown away.

Keep her safe, Lord. Please keep her safe.

TEN

A scream pierced the air.

Holly peeked out through the window and spotted Mason heading her way. But he wasn't alone. In his arms, he was dragging a kicking and screaming woman. At first, Holly couldn't tell who she was, but as he drew closer she saw a familiar face—Sherri Livingston. Despite her struggling, she was no match for Mason's strength and no one in the building seemed inclined to step in to help. Her ire flared. She'd hoped they'd gotten through to Sherri and she'd gone into hiding with her daughter. How had Mason tracked her down? Now she was Mason's prisoner just as Holly was.

"Mason, please don't hurt me," Sherri cried when he stepped inside, pulling her along with him. "Please, Mason. I have a daughter. She needs me. Please let me go. I won't betray you again. I promise I won't."

"Shut up!" Mason bellowed then plopped her down into a chair beside Holly and bound her hands with another set of zip-ties. Once secure, he stepped back and glanced at them, a smug smile curving his lips. "The boss wants to talk to you both. Then you'll be begging me to put a bullet through your head once he's done with you."

Sherri's eyes widened in fear and she sobbed again. "Please, Mason. I'm sorry."

He turned away from her and looked at Holly then knelt beside her. He reached out and touched Holly's face, moving a finger down her cheek. "We could have been good together, Holly."

His touch repulsed her and she jutted her chin and glared at him. "Don't touch me. I would never be with you, Mason Webber. You killed Jimmy. You disgust me."

"Jimmy didn't know when to keep his nose out of other people's business. Apparently it's something you two had in common."

Sherri continued her pleading. "Mason, please, tell him I've been good. I did everything you asked of me. Please don't let him kill me. Who'll take care of my daughter if I die?"

Mason seemed untouched by her pleading. He sneered at Sherri. "You should have thought of that before you went blabbing to these two. You're on your own with the boss."

He walked out, closed and locked the door, then glanced at them both as if to reassure himself they were secure before he vanished from the window.

When he was out of sight, Holly started pulling at her bindings while Sherri sobbed behind her, all hope lost. "Sherri, we have to get out of here before he returns with the boss. See if you can pull your hands free."

"I can't." Sherri's voice was hopeless and whiny. She'd given up already.

"Think about your daughter," Holly told her. "You have to get free for her sake."

She sniffed back a few tears, but the sobbing seemed to stop and Holly could tell she was reaching the younger woman. "What's your daughter's name?"

"Melissa. She's four."

"I'll bet she's precious."

"She is. I love her so much. I don't know what's going to happen to her."

"Nothing is going to happen to her. We're going to get out of here. Keep pulling on those bindings."

Sherri nodded and started pulling, but gave up after only a moment and whined again. "It's no use. We're doomed."

"We are not. I'm not dying here today." She glanced around the room searching for something sharp to cut the zip-tie with, but the room was pretty well cleared out of belongings. All that remained were empty shelves, the desk and chairs. But maybe the corner of the desk could do the job. She tried to stand and discovered Mason had looped the tie to her chair. She didn't let that stop her. She hopped over to the desk and tried to position herself so she could use the edge of the desk to cut the line.

"Watch the window," she commanded Sherri. "If you see them heading this way, let me know."

Sherri sniffed back tears again but she nodded and glanced at the window. Holly thought she would remain levelheaded now that she had her daughter to fight for.

She knew what it was like to fight for someone you cared about.

Her mind wandered to Blake. He was most likely safe now that the helicopter had flown away. She was glad, but some part of her wondered if she should have fought harder for him. It felt wrong to have him accuse her of conspiring with Mason and the chief, but now as she thought about it, she couldn't blame him. But she could never build a life with someone who didn't trust her completely.

A rush of excitement burst through her when she felt the plastic give way and her hands were free. She pulled the zip-ties away then began digging through the drawers to try to find something to use to cut Sherri free. They had to get out before Mason returned and brought the boss with him. In a bottom drawer, she found a box cutter and hurried to Sherri, quickly cutting through the thick plastic.

"Let's get out of here before they come back," she said. "Stay low, but if you see anyone, run."

Sherri nodded her understanding then squeezed Holly's hand. "Thank you," she said.

Holly squeezed her hand back. "Let's get you back to your daughter."

She opened the door and peered out, glancing around for some sort of guard, but there was none. Apparently, Mason thought tying them to chairs was enough to keep them from escaping. A smug feeling rushed through her. He would regret underestimating Holly. She took Sherri's hand and moved toward an open doorway. She had no idea where they were going or what they would do once they were out. All she was focusing on was getting out of this building without being seen.

God, please help us.

Her prayer must have reached His ears because the area was clear. Sunlight filtered in through the windows, casting shadows around the building. Holly heard voices in the distance but they seemed to be in the opposite direction. The door was only a few feet away. She squeezed Sherri's hand and pulled her as she moved toward the door. Excitement bubbled through her as they neared it. They were going to make it!

She reached out for the handle then stopped short when she heard Mason's voice right outside.

She backed away slowly. They would have to find another way out. She motioned Sherri to turn and head for the other door. She wasn't giving up, no matter what. She was determined to escape Mason's grasp.

Sherri's hand slipped from hers and Holly heard a squeal from behind her. She turned and saw Sherri stumble into a stack of boxes. She plowed into them headfirst and they clattered to the floor, making a loud racket Holly was certain Mason would hear.

Sure enough, moments later, the doors swung open and Mason and several others ran inside.

"Run!" Holly screeched and pulled Sherri to her feet. They headed to another door on the back wall.

Shots rang out and Sherri screamed, but Holly didn't let up. She pulled on her hand to keep her moving before fear planted her feet. Mason would surely kill them both if he caught them. "Don't stop," she told Sherri. "Keep running."

She screamed again as the men continued to fire shots at them that hit the concrete walls and bounced off, cracking through the crates. She reached the secondary doors, grabbing the handle. It didn't budge. The doors were locked. She pushed at them and kicked, trying to break open the doors, but she couldn't.

Behind her, Sherri was gasping and trying to catch her breath. "What do we do now?"

She glanced around the area. Until they could find another way out, there was only one thing they could do. "We hide."

Sherri ran into the next room and Holly followed her. The tables and the equipment, but mostly the putrid smell, alerted her that this was most likely where they cooked the chemicals. She covered her mouth and nose with her hand, but found a desk to climb under while Sherri hid behind a stack of boxes.

The smell, the impending threat of death and Sherri's soft sobs were all more than Holly could stand. Once she was still, reality seemed to sink in. They weren't going to make it out of there alive. Even if they managed to escape the building, where could they go? They were miles from town and the police force was corrupt.

She closed her eyes and allowed a tear to slip down her face. This wasn't how she wanted things to end. She wished she could tell Blake again she loved him, because she did. It didn't matter that it had only been a few days or that she hardly knew him. She knew the man he was...a godly man whose mission in life was to protect those in need. He was a true hero.

She let her mind wander to what might have been and

wished they'd had the opportunity to see what kind of future they could have together. But she realized something else, too. There was someone else she needed to make amends with—God. She'd held on to her bitterness and anger so fiercely, but Blake had helped her to see that God was not her enemy. He wasn't the one who'd taken everything from her. But He could have been the one to restore it all. And she believed it. She didn't have to be perfect or completely ready to forgive. She only needed to let go of her anger and turn back to God. Blake had told her that it didn't matter how you came back to God, only that you returned to Him. He was willing to take her back without the clear soul or sparkling life. She had nothing to prove to God and everything to gain. She only wished she'd given Him that chance sooner.

Footsteps growing closer grabbed her attention and Holly's stomach plummeted. There were only so many places to hide in this shop and Mason had to know they had come into this room. From her hiding spot, she could still hear Sherri's soft sobs and tried to motion to her to quiet down. Sherri saw her and nodded her understanding, but she didn't seem able to stop the sobbing. Mason, or whoever was in the room with them, had to hear her. But it was too late. Mason stepped between them, grabbed Sherri by her hair and dragged her from behind the boxes.

Dread filled her as Sherri screamed out in fear.

Mason dug his gun into her neck and snarled. "Did you really think you could get away from me, Sherri?"

Holly quickly realized that he hadn't seen her yet.

Maybe there was a way she could help Sherri before he found her. She scanned the room and spotted a shelf filled with large jars. She didn't know what they were used for, but she suspected one of them over the head would take down even a man as big as Mason. If only she could reach them before Mason pulled that trigger. She didn't know if he was bluffing, still waiting on the boss, or if he might shoot at any moment and kill Sherri right then and there.

With his back to her, Holly slid from under the desk and quickly but quietly padded across the floor. She couldn't see Sherri's face, but the panic in her voice as she begged Mason to spare her was obvious.

Holly grabbed one of the jars then ran at Mason. He must have heard her because he turned just as she reached him. As he raised the gun at her, she slammed the jar against Mason's head. The glass shattered and splattered. Mason cried out in pain. His knees buckled and he hit the ground, landing on top of Sherri. The gun slipped through his hand and slid across the floor. Holly tried to grab it but it slid beneath a table. She dropped to her knees and tried to reach for it, but it was too far back.

Holly glanced at Sherri, who was sobbing and trying to pull herself free of an unconscious Mason. His body weight had her leg pinned and Holly noticed he was starting to move. He would be waking up soon.

She left the gun and ran to Sherri. "Let's get out of here," Holly said, pulling her leg out from under his bulky weight.

They ran toward the front entrance, determined they

would make it out this time while Mason was unconscious and the others were searching the building for them. But Sherri was already limping beside her, favoring the foot that Mason had landed on, and couldn't run as fast as Holly would have liked. She draped one of Sherri's arms over her shoulder to carry some of her weight.

Just before they reached them, the doors burst open and two men grabbed Holly and Sherri. She kicked at them and struggled although she knew it was fruitless. A moment later she spotted Mason emerging from the cooking room, blood dripping down his head. He was holding it, too. She had felt the jar slam into his head and knew how hard it had been. But her only regret was that it hadn't knocked him out long enough for them to escape.

The men forced them back into the room and into the same chairs they'd previously been tied to.

"Bind her hands and feet," Mason ordered the men, motioning to Sherri. He walked to the filing cabinet and pulled out a first-aid kit, slamming it onto the desk. He locked eyes with Holly. "You bandage me up."

She started to protest that she wouldn't touch his head, but he incentivized his request by pulling out his gun and raising it to Sherri's face. He must have found it underneath the table.

"I'll kill her if you refuse."

She glanced at Sherri then conceded.

Mason dropped into the chair she'd previously occupied while Holly opened the medical kit and got to work cleaning up Mason's wounds. She picked shards of glass from his head and he grimaced and gripped at the gun in his lap each time she dug for a piece of glass. She needed appropriate instruments and he needed stitches. Without them, he would have a scar. It sort of pleased her to think Mason would have a scar on his head that would always remind him of how Holly had bested him.

"The boss has gone to check on the lockdown situation with Chief Waggoner. When he returns, it'll be time to take care of you both and I hope he lets me be the one to do it."

The bitterness in his voice bit at Holly. He was the one who'd destroyed her life and murdered her husband, yet his tone suggested he'd been the one put upon. She bit back a bitter tirade, knowing it would do nothing but enrage him further.

She glanced at Sherri, who returned her gaze with questioning hope. She had no idea when he would return, but she knew it would be too soon for her. The longer they could remain alive, the greater opportunity Blake had of rescuing them. She knew he would return for her just as surely as she knew his eyes were the color of the sky. He would come. Her job was to remain alive until he did.

Blake pored over the map of Northshore that Matt had secured and laid across a table inside the offices of the DEA. There had to be another way into that town, but the water was a major obstacle. Colton and Garrett had worked up a plan to go by speedboat and were out trying to get their hands on one while Josh was glued to the police scanner trying to glean any details from the roadblocks.

Blake was just trying to wrap his head around the fact that he'd left Holly there and beating himself up for allowing Mason to ambush him the way he had. He'd never forget the look on Holly's face as she'd slipped through his fingers.

Matt appeared in the doorway. "Find anything yet?"

"No," Blake said. "Nothing better than the speed-boat plan, anyway."

"I may have a better plan." He walked over to a video monitor and pressed a button, lighting up a plan Matt had been working on for the DEA to breach the town if the time came. Blake had seen it and thought it would work if they could ever get the go-ahead from Matt's bosses.

"It's a good plan, but it takes more guns and people than we'll have. Sneaking back into town is still our best option."

Matt grinned. "Not anymore. The DEA has officially ended negotiations with Chief Waggoner."

A strange mix of excitement and trepidation burst through Blake, but he tempered it. "Are you telling me that the DEA is breaching the town?"

"Yes, I am. And better yet, they've put me in charge of the infiltration. I'm putting together a team to go in and I want you on it, Blake."

Relief flooded through him at the news he'd waited so long to hear. He'd fought so long and hard to escape Northshore and now he was going back there. He only hoped Holly could hold on until he arrived.

* * *

Mason's phone buzzed at his hip and he lifted it to glance at the screen. His body tensed and he pushed Holly's hand away and stood. "The boss is back," he said to his men. He looked down at the bandage and gauze wrappers on the desk and growled. "The boss is here and this place looks like a mess." He spun and faced Holly. "This is all your fault," he growled then backhanded her across the mouth.

Pain riddled through her and the desk was the only thing that kept her from hitting the floor. She dropped the gauze and tape she'd been using to bandage his wound and pressed her hand to her jaw to try to stop the sting.

Mason paced like an angry lion on the hunt, moving from one side of Sherri to the other. He held the gun in his hand and she watched him go back and forth. She expected him to shoot her, but Holly knew he wouldn't. It wasn't his call anymore. Mason Webber answered to someone even more evil than him. And that person was on his way inside right now.

She heard footsteps approaching and gasped at who she saw through the glass. Moments later, the door into the room swung open and the person behind the drugs, the deaths, and Mason stepped inside.

"Gabriel." She gasped, her mind unable to comprehend how he could be standing there in front of her. "But I—I saw you get shot. I saw you drown."

His mouth curved into a mischievous grin. "Yes, you did, and thank you for that, Holly. Too many people were getting a little too close to finding out I was in charge of this entire operation. When you and Blake showed up on my doorstep, you offered me the perfect escape. Death."

Her mind whirled at the possibility.

"While I was out of the room pretending to call Blake's DEA friend, I placed a call to Mason here. I had him set the entire thing up. I figured if I were dead, no one would come looking for me, would they?"

"But Blake said you were working with Mayor Banks to clean up the city."

"I was working with Mayor Banks to keep my nose clean and to make certain her investigation never went anywhere. After all, I couldn't give her reason to fire Chief Waggoner, could I? She might discover he was on my payroll all along."

"So you killed her?"

"Unfortunately, your and Blake's investigation has created problems for me, Holly. Problems with the locals, problems with the state police, problems with the DEA waiting on the other side of the bridge, just itching for a reason to come in here and take over my city. I had such a good thing going, too."

Holly balked. "You had a good thing going? You're selling poison to children. It doesn't get any lower than that, Gabriel."

"I'm a businessman, Holly. Or at least, I used to be. Now I'm dead and living off the fruits of my labor. I can see we're done in Northshore, though. This town has been compromised so now we'll have to find another place to set up shop."

She shook her head. "Blake will stop you. He'll figure all this out and he will track you down."

"Not me. No one is even looking for me, Holly. I'm a ghost. And, unfortunately, in order to stay that way, I can't leave anyone alive who has seen me not dead."

Sherri's sobs started again but Holly remained silent. She wouldn't beg for her life because she knew the only reason Gabriel had come here was that he'd planned to kill her all along.

"No, please," Sherri begged, tears streaming down her face. "I have a daughter. Please, I won't tell anyone about you. I promise."

"Shut up!" Mason yelled then slapped her. "You already proved you can't be trusted when you talked to Blake and told him all about our operation."

"I didn't," she said, pleading. "I didn't tell him."

"Then how did he know where we were?" Holly smirked, causing Mason to glare at her. "What's so funny?"

"Sherri didn't know anything about this place. It was Jimmy. He led us here."

He looked confused. "Jimmy?"

"His journal specifically. He followed you here one night and he wrote it down. Blake is the one who figured it all out."

"Blake Michaels had you figured out real quick, Mason," Gabriel said. "He knew you didn't have enough brains in your head to pull off an operation like this. He played you and you allowed it."

"I did not."

"Face it, he bested you."

Mason's face reddened. He grabbed Holly and pulled her to her feet then jabbed the gun into her head. "He didn't look like a victor when I yanked his girlfriend right out of his arms as the helicopter was taking off."

"Maybe so, but he'll be back with reinforcements. We can't be here when he does. Close this shop down and start shipping these containers to the Oklahoma plant. We're relocating. You have one hour." He got up and started walking for the door then stopped to give Mason one last instruction. "Kill them and dump their bodies."

Gabriel vanished through the doors and the other men followed him, leaving Mason alone in the room with them. Sherri's cries and pleading started again, but Mason's expression was stoic. He cut her binds, then pulled her from the chair and dragged her kicking and screaming from the room. Holly leaped up and grabbed his arm, trying futilely to stop him. He shoved her and she went tumbling backward, hitting the chair and then the floor. The door slammed shut, but Holly could still hear Sherri's cries. A gunshot moments later silenced her. Horror raced through Holly along with fear and dread as she heard someone approach the door. She glanced around, hoping in vain to find some way of escape, but she was trapped. The door opened and Mason walked back inside, gun still in hand.

She saw no remorse in his expression. It didn't bother him at all to shoot Sherri and then her. How many others had he killed? She shook away that thought, realizing she didn't really want to know. She knew now with absolute certainty that he was a killer.

She didn't want her last thoughts to be of Mason. She

allowed another image to slip into her mind's eye. Sitting on the pier with Blake in the moonlight and the feel of the cool water on her feet and his arm wrapped tightly around her. She smiled. It was a good last thought to have.

Mason raised the gun and Holly grimaced.

Take care, Blake, her heart cried. He deserved to find someone who would realize what an amazing man he truly was. *Heal his scars, Lord. And help him to find love again.*

She closed her eyes and waited to hear the click of the gun then braced herself for the end.

It didn't come.

Instead she heard a low thump, thump, thump fill the air. Her eyes shot open. It was the helicopter returning!

Mason had heard it, too, and ran to the window to look out. He swore then turned back to Holly, but she was through kowtowing to him. She picked up the chair he'd forgotten to strap her to and smashed it over his head just as she had the jar. His knees gave out and he slipped. She raised the chair again, slamming it even harder this time. Mason hit the floor and groaned.

When the gun slipped from his hand, Holly dropped the chair, snatched up the gun and ran, heading for the doors, determined to make it this time. But before she reached the doors, an explosion sent her reeling.

Blake leaped from the DEA helicopter at the sound of the blast. Panic burst through him. They'd only just arrived when the explosion occurred and he had no idea what had caused it. Was Holly still inside that building? And had she been anywhere near the blast?

Matt's hand on his shoulder stopped him before his urge to burst inside overcame him. "We'll find her."

Blake found confidence in his friend's reassurance but he knew the truth. He'd been gone for hours. Mason could have moved Holly somewhere else by now...or worse, killed her. He pushed back that thought. He would find her and once he did, he would never let her go again.

Matt signaled to the other DEA agents who'd arrived with them in the chopper to surround the building and sweep it for survivors. Blake readied his weapon and followed Matt, who kicked in the front door and ran inside. Blake came up behind him and flanked him. Scorch marks were evident on the floor and walls, indicating a recent explosion. Blake kicked away debris as he moved through the repair shop, his eyes scanning for both Mason's men and any sign of Holly.

"I found something in the back office," a voice said over the radio in his ear. Matt moved in that direction and Blake did, too. As he approached the agent who'd made the call, he noticed a woman's figure lying on the concrete floor.

His heart raced at the sight of dark hair. *Please no, Lord.* He hurried over and saw it wasn't Holly after all. His racing pulse began to slow as he knelt beside the familiar figure.

"Her name was Sherri Livingston," he told the men. Mason had finally tied up that loose end.

But where was Holly?

Another call came over his earpiece. "We found a body."

Blake held his breath until they announced the details. "It's a man's body. Looks like he died in the blast."

Blake let out a sigh of relief that it wasn't her. At least that was something.

He heard a groan coming from a corner and rushed over, moving several pieces of debris. He spotted a leg and movement and knew someone was pinned beneath the rubble.

"Hang on," he said, pushing away several pieces of paneling to reveal a familiar but unexpected face. "Gabriel!" He grabbed the man's hand and pulled him free. His knees wobbled but he managed to get on his feet. Blake couldn't help the surprise that filled him. "I thought—I mean, I saw Mason shoot you."

"Yes, he did shoot me, but he only wounded me. He's kept me a prisoner here in this awful place ever since. You have to find Mason and stop him. He's a maniac."

"You don't need to worry about Mason anymore. We'll find him. We've already located one man killed in the explosion. Any idea what caused it?"

"I don't know. There are a lot of chemicals inside this building. Perhaps one of them combusted."

Blake heard movement a few feet away and turned toward it. His heart lurched when he spotted someone under more debris. That could be Holly.

He turned back to tell Gabriel to stay put, but when he did, Gabriel had a knife in his hand. He lunged at Blake with it.

Pain riddled through Holly as she dragged herself back to consciousness. Every inch of her hurt but a heavy weight seemed to be holding her down. She forced her eyes open and tried to glance around, realizing a large cabinet had fallen on top of her, pinning her legs beneath it.

She felt around her and touched the cold metal of the gun. She still had it. Good. But now she needed to get free of the cabinet.

She heard footsteps and froze. Was it Mason coming to find her? Voices rose and then there was the sound of a scuffle. She couldn't see and was afraid to even try to look for fear of alerting Mason to her whereabouts, but she needed to know if it was him coming after her.

She lifted her head and strained to look over a pile of debris blocking her view. She still couldn't see, but recognized Blake's voice the moment she heard it. He'd returned for her! That realization gave her new strength and she managed to free one leg. The other was still stuck, but it was enough for her to twist and turn to see over the pile of junk. It was Blake. He was dressed in gear similar to what his friends had been wearing earlier and he was in the middle of a hand-to-knife fight with another man. Gabriel. Blake would have been as shocked to see him alive as she'd been and she imagined Gabriel used that to his advantage to pull the knife on Blake.

The two men were now locked together in some sort of stranglehold and Holly could see Blake was struggling to keep the knife from cutting him. She scrambled to grab the gun and pull herself into a position to shoot it, but her right foot remained trapped beneath the cabinet, restricting her movement.

Please, God, help me.

She couldn't do this herself and she had to get free. She had to free herself and help him.

The two men continued their struggle and so did Holly, freeing herself inch by inch. Finally she managed to turn and face Blake and Gabriel. She raised the gun and aimed it, but finding her target was difficult when the two men were so close together. She wanted to call out, but her throat was raw and hoarse from the explosion and the smoke in the air. All she managed to do was cough and neither man heard her.

She aimed the gun again. Firing it would grab their attention and possibly open up a shot for her. She raised the gun again to fire, but a hand grabbed hers from behind.

"Not so fast, Holly." He ripped the gun from her hand then kicked at the cabinet restraining her and pulled her to her feet. Pain ripped through her ankle when she tried to place her weight on it. "You're coming with me."

He wrapped his arm around her neck and literally dragged her across the floor, her ankle screaming the entire way.

Blake spotted their movement. "Hey, let her go!" he shouted but Mason didn't stop and Holly saw Blake take a hit from Gabriel. And the last thing she saw before Mason pulled her out the door was Blake falling to his knees.

Blake winced at the blow Gabriel had given him but he didn't let it stop him. He spun around as Gabriel lunged with the knife again. But Blake had a renewed determination. He'd seen Holly being dragged away by Mason and he wouldn't let her go again. He kicked the knife from Gabriel's hand then leaped to his feet and tackled him. Gabriel hit the wall then slid to the floor, holding his head. He'd put up a good fight for a guy who was supposed to be dead, but Blake figured that had all been a ruse for their benefit. Obviously, Gabriel was working with Mason. But why the charade?

Blake retrieved his rifle from where it had fallen then pulled a zip-tie from one of his pockets and bound Gabriel's hands.

"It's not too late, Blake. You can still be a part of this. There's a lot of money to be had in this operation and it can be yours. All you have to do is let me go."

Understanding dawned on Blake. "You faked your death because you were the one behind this drug ring."

"Do you really think Mason has the brains to pull something like this off? I've got six factories all cranking this stuff out. Mason couldn't even keep one of them protected."

"Well, your operation is officially shut down," Blake said. He clicked on his radio and called to Matt. "I found your ring leader. It's Gabriel Butler."

Confusion was evident in Matt's response. "Isn't he dead?"

"Not anymore. You'll find him by the front entrance. I'm going after Mason. He ran out the back door and he has Holly."

"I'll send someone to get Gabriel and I'll meet you at the back."

Blake ran toward the back door and burst through it,

gun raised and ready to fire. He wouldn't let Mason get away with Holly again. This was ending today.

He spotted Mason pulling her around a corner.

"Stop!" Blake called, raising his weapon and ready to fire.

Mason spun around and put the gun to Holly's head. "Don't come any closer," he demanded. "We're getting in that truck and we're getting out of here."

Blake shook his head. "That's not happening. Let her go, Mason. Let's end this right now."

"I've got the girl, Blakey. I've got the upper hand again. I win."

"You can't win this, Mason. The DEA has this town locked down. Chief Waggoner has been arrested and Gabriel is tied up inside. It's over."

Mason jabbed the gun at Holly's temple to make his point, but Blake could see he was racking his brain for a way out and wouldn't just surrender peacefully. This was going to end bloody. He may have no choice but to shoot, regardless of how close Holly was to him.

Lord, guide my hand.

He was usually a good shot but his hands were shaking with fear that Holly would be ripped from him again. He couldn't stand losing her, especially since he hadn't had a chance to assure her he trusted her completely. Blake heard Colton's calm voice. "I've got my sights set on him."

He nearly breathed a sigh of relief. Colton's hands were steady and he had a sniper's aim. He could take out Mason if necessary.

"I've also got a shot," Garrett echoed through the earpiece.

"Ditto," called Josh.

At the same time Matt rushed through the door along with a pair of heavily armed agents.

Having the Rangers on his side, knowing they were there for him, bolstered Blake's confidence. They could take out Mason...only he didn't know if they could do it before he shot and killed Holly.

He kept that lingering doubt out of his voice. "You can't win this, Mason. You're surrounded."

He tightened his arm around Holly's neck. Her eyes were wide with fear, but Blake tried to reassure her with his tone that everything would be fine.

"We can work this out. We already know Gabriel was the one in charge. You were just following orders."

Mason spotted the guns trained on him.

Blake saw panic rising in him and sensed things were about to get interesting.

Suddenly, Blake saw Holly jab her elbow into Mason's stomach. He doubled over and released his grip on her. She didn't hesitate before slipping through and hightailing it toward Blake.

Mason saw her and raised his gun, but they all had a clear shot on him now.

Blake fired and heard several other shots ring out, as well, before Mason could even pull the trigger on his gun. His body shook, riddled with bullets, for several seconds before he hit the ground. This time, he didn't get up.

Holly ran to Blake and fell into his arms. He swept

her up and sighed with relief and a flood of emotions he couldn't even verbalize. He cupped her face and kissed her long and hard until another voice from the sea of men spoke via the earpiece.

"Don't get any closer to the building. The sparks you two are emitting could set this whole place ablaze in a heartbeat."

Blake broke away then gave an embarrassed look at his friend. "Very funny, Colton."

"Hey, that's no joke. The two of you are a fire hazard."

He stroked her face and smiled, a smile that ran so deep he'd never known he could feel so much love for one person. "You're too late," he told Colton. "The blaze is already a raging inferno." He pulled his hand through her hair and stared into her eyes. "I'm so sorry I ever doubted you, Holly. I was being stupid and irrational. I know you would never betray me."

"I wouldn't."

"I tried to come back for you sooner. I got here as soon as I could."

"I know. You came just in time. Mason had the gun to my head. I thought I was about to die."

Her words stung him like a thousand bug bites and he groused angrily. Why hadn't he returned sooner?

"My last thought was of you, Blake Michaels, and how much I love you." She touched his face and her voice choked. "I thought I would never get to see you again. I love you. I know it's quick and I know you might think we don't know one another well enough yet, but I won't deny it anymore."

"I love you, too, Holly Mathis. You're right. It is too soon and we hardly know each other, but I never want to spend another moment apart from you. Will you marry me?"

It seemed her entire body was full of joy, so much so that it wouldn't even contain it. She smiled and nodded, barely able to speak. "I will," she finally managed to squeak out between her tears. "I would love to marry you. Now take me in your arms and kiss me."

He thought his heart would burst from his chest with the wellspring of happiness that flooded him. In an instant he knew that anything he'd ever felt for Miranda paled in comparison to his love for Holly. This was real. This was true love. "Yes, ma'am," he said then pulled her into his arms and kissed her long and lovingly.

This was where he wanted to be and it couldn't be more perfect.

EPILOGUE

Holly stared in awe at the colors that lined the sky as the sun set on a perfect day. She'd celebrated with Blake at the wedding of his friends Colton and Laura. They, as well as the other Rangers and their wives and girl-friends, had made her feel so welcome and accepted into their obviously tight-knit group. Now she was standing on Blake's back porch in Compton, Louisiana, watching God show off His creativity. It all seemed a far cry from only two weeks ago when they'd been fighting for their lives in Northshore.

She sensed Blake's presence as he emerged from the house and wrapped his arms around her. She leaned into his protective embrace. This was where she wanted to live, right here in his arms, but she couldn't. She had to make plans for her future.

She hadn't set foot back in Northshore since the fed-eral government had swooped in and taken over the town. Chief Waggoner had been arrested along with Gabriel and twenty-eight other people found culpable in the drug manufacturing and distribution organization.

And the corruption hadn't been limited to the police force, either. The DEA had uncovered evidence naming local businessmen, tourist facilities and even high-level hospital employees. It broke her heart to realize her town had been infected with corruption and that it had prevailed for so long. Jimmy had seen it and fought against it and now, thanks to Blake, it had been stamped out. But the town was a shell of what it had once been and Holly knew their tourism would take a hit next year. The only bright spot was that Pastor Dave had been released unharmed from the jail when the agents had taken over.

Truthfully, she didn't even know if she wanted to return. Her life there had also been decimated, yet she had to admit that God had already started the healing process. He was truly repaying her for what had been taken.

She turned and stared up into Blake's face. She didn't know what her future held, but she knew she wanted this man to be a part of it. She hoped he felt the same way. He'd asked her to marry him two weeks ago after the ordeal with Mason had ended, but he hadn't mentioned it again. Had he misspoke in the heat of the moment? Or had he changed his mind completely?

He examined her now. "What are you thinking about so intently?" he asked.

Embarrassment caused her face to flush. Didn't he know she was always thinking of him? "I was wondering about my future. I need to start making some plans."

He nodded. "I was thinking about that, too."

"You were?"

He nodded. "The DEA offered me a job working as

a field agent, but it would require me to be gone most of the time working undercover."

Her heart fell but she tried not to let it show in her expression. He was going to take another dangerous assignment and be gone for months on end. She'd known this was the kind of man he was yet she wasn't prepared for the stab at her heart his plans caused her. But she couldn't let him know how it affected her. She hadn't wanted to fall for a risk-taker again, but she had. Now she had to live with her choice. She steadied her voice. "That sounds like a great opportunity for you."

He touched her face, his finger playing with a wisp of hair on her forehead. "It would be…if I were going to accept it. I'm not. Trust me, I've had my fill of undercover work. Too many secrets to keep. I prefer the transparency of good, honest police work." He gave her a wry smile. "And I just so happen to know there's a job opening for chief of police in Northshore."

The elation she felt only moments ago faded. "Wait, you want to go back to Northshore?"

"You don't?"

"I don't know. I'm not sure. That town took so much from me. How can it ever feel like home again?"

"It's up to us to make it a home, Holly. There's a lot of rebuilding of trust to be done. Bitterness and hopelessness were so much a part of life there for so long. It'll be hard to believe in anything else, but I have faith that we can make a difference there."

He pulled away from her. "But I won't go without you. From now on, wherever we go, we go together." He reached into his pocket and pulled out something.

Her breath caught when she realized it was a ring. "I asked you a very important question a while back and you said yes. I hope your answer hasn't changed."

Hot, happy tears threatened her eyes as she looked up into his blue eyes and saw the only future she cared about—a future as a wife to this man. "It hasn't," she whispered. "I love you, Blake, and if you're going back to Northshore, then so am I."

He slipped the ring on her finger and she leaned into him for a kiss that sealed their future. In that moment she knew God had truly restored to her what the locusts ate. And with hard work and faith, she knew He could restore her town, as well, and make it a place she and Blake could call home.

* * * * *

If you liked this story, pick up these other
RANGERS UNDER FIRE *books*
by Virginia Vaughan:

YULETIDE ABDUCTION
REUNION MISSION
RANCH REFUGE
MISTLETOE REUNION THREAT

Available now from Love Inspired!

Find more great reads at www.LoveInspired.com

Dear Reader,

After I wrote *Ranch Refuge*, I had many people ask me if Blake would get his own story. I was happy to tell them he would! I loved giving Blake his second chance at love in *Mission Undercover*. Only, after his fiancée's bitter betrayal, Blake is struggling to trust anyone, especially himself.

Usually we get into our biggest messes by relying on our own judgment instead of listening for God's guidance. Proverbs 3:5–6 reminds us to "Trust in the Lord with all your heart and lean not on your own understanding; in all your ways submit to Him, and He will make your paths straight." It's a truth we all need to be reminded of from time to time.

I love hearing from my readers! You can contact me through my website, virginiavaughanonline.com, or through the publisher.

Blessings!
Virginia